CONTENTS

This book is dedicated to
all those courageous enough to chase their dreams.

Gina Hooten Popp

10/28/18

Up Near Dallas

Gina Hooten Popp

ISBN-13: 978-0997955859
ISBN-10: 0997955856

ACKNOWLEDGMENTS

My gratitude goes to my family and friends for their support during the writing of this story. I would especially like to thank my mother Peggie Hooten for all of her help and advice.

PROLOGUE

Dallas, Texas

Monday Afternoon

March 19, 1934

DR. JEROME LYLES

There are some pains of the body that modern medicine can't heal. The strain on the heart of my best friend and mentor was unbearable. I wanted to step in and help, but I knew the outcome would depend on him. Only he could bring himself back from the brink.

Through observation, I've found, it is those we love most who are capable of inflicting a pain so deep there's almost no recovering from it—especially when the tormentor is your own flesh and blood.

Yet there was nothing I could say to my friend Lucky McLaren, or his wayward son Mick, to make them reconnect, to force them to understand each other. For they were cut from two different cloths. Different enough that they stood independent in thought and appearance, yet sufficiently similar that they couldn't let go of the bond between them.

This morning, I found Mick walking up the road to my house after he'd hopped a freight train from Houston last night. The trek must have exhausted him, as the closest train tracks to us were four miles away. And, of course, he hadn't had the foresight to bring any food with him

1

when he'd stormed out of his father's house. So, he was hungry as a wolf. I heard his stomach rumbling as we stood talking.

Once I got Mick safely inside the door of my modest frame home, my wife Olivia set about fussing over him, feeding him and asking if he wanted a warm bath before he stretched out for a nap. Fretting was second nature to her; it was how she showed her love—and Mick seemed to love her back for it. They didn't have expectations of each other and didn't place any hope on one another. Therefore, they got along famously. Ahh, but that's how it goes.

After he'd polished off the sandwich and cider she'd set out for him, Olivia shooed him off to the bathhouse. "Did you notice how much he resembles his father?" she whispered into my ear before she went to prepare the little guest room off the kitchen for him.

Without answering her directly, I said, "Tell him he's welcome to stay as long as he wants."

Putting on my glasses, I looked for the notes that contained my patients' telephone exchanges and numbers. I took my glasses off again before wiping a tear from the corner of my eye. I needed to call my friend and tell him his son Mick was with me. I knew he'd be worried sick, and I didn't want him to have one more moment of anguish. How could it be that Lucky McLaren had taught me so many lessons, yet he wasn't open to learning a universal truth from me in return? I shook my head.

"Jerome," Olivia called from the doorway. "Come and give me a hand with these sheets. The job is much easier with two people."

"Let me call Mick's parents first."

Olivia moved to the doorway and watched as I picked up the phone and spoke with an operator, who informed me the line was busy.

"You can try again later," Olivia said. "If they don't call first, looking for him."

1 HINDSIGHT IS 20/20

Dallas, Texas

Tuesday Afternoon

March 20, 1934

MARGARET

I hung onto the side of the Model T for dear life as the warm breeze rushed past my face. Looking down at the running board, I could make out the embossed word "FORD." March in Texas was hot, but not overbearing. I could have walked home from school. Instead, I was riding in style—and boy-o-boy was it funner than just about anything I'd experienced in my fifteen years on this earth.

My thick hair blew wildly as it came loose from its long braid. Mama was going to be hopping mad when she saw me; she was constantly accusing me of being a tomboy, and now I was proving her point. Mama would also tell me "funner" was not a real word. To heck with my mother and her rules.

The red-haired woman in the passenger seat cautioned the driver. "Don't go too fast, Bud." I couldn't help but admire how fashionable she looked with her mouth colored in the latest shade of daring red. Her smile was friendly and inviting. Before she spoke, I would've guessed she was down from New York City, but then I heard her faint Texas accent and I suspected she grew up somewhere around Dallas.

"Shoot, I'm not going too fast." The man slowed his speed to a crawl and yelled at me through the open window. "You got a tight grip, girl?"

I nodded my head as hair whipped in front of my eyes. Shyly, I studied the couple inside the automobile. Their sophistication made me feel nervous and unsure of myself. Though he didn't have classic good looks, the man had a persuasive charm about him. And he was a fancy dresser too, in his store-bought suit. I wondered what these two made of my homemade school clothes.

Why earlier, when they'd pull up alongside of me walking and asked if I knew of a place where they could rent a couple rooms, I was surprised to find myself answering. "No hotels or motels this far out in the country, but perhaps my daddy will let you stay in one of the empty cabins he keeps for farm workers. They aren't much to look at, but they're clean and comfortable inside."

I knew it was a bad idea as soon as the words tumbled out of my mouth. But since I'd already said it, I felt I had to follow through on the offer.

At that point in the conversation, the couple asked me to get in their car so they could ride me home and talk to my daddy. But I told them Daddy had a rule that us children were not to get in cars with strangers.

The man—Bud was his name—figured if I rode on the sideboard it wouldn't really be getting in the car, and I wouldn't get in trouble. He argued it just wouldn't be right leaving me to walk while they rode ahead. And I could see his point, even though I knew Daddy probably wouldn't.

My parents weren't the kind of folks that took kindly to strangers. Not that we ever had very many strangers stopping by. In fact, I think I've known everyone in our near vicinity my whole life.

"I live up the road just apiece," I hollered though the passenger window. "Turn left at that big oak tree." Looking up, I admired the green leaves providing a canopy of shade along the way. As I clung to the automobile, I thought of what I'd say when we pulled up to the house. Probably be best to wing it and respond to what my parents said first, I figured.

I was happy to see the driver navigating around the holes in the road, so as not to bounce me off. Part black top and part gravel, the old road to our house had seen more than its fair share of potholes. Perhaps these two people I was bringing home would be a blessing to our family. I didn't know why Daddy had to be so suspicious of everyone, but I guessed it was related to the hard times going around the country. People were doing things they ordinarily wouldn't, just to eat and get the basic necessities of life. My mother said these were some of the worst times people had ever seen in the United States.

A dog barked, and I caught a glimpse of it as it ran onto the road from the field. I wasn't afraid, it was just a blue heeler stray my brother had adopted. She looked fierce, but I knew she was a cream puff. Once she realized it was me hanging on the side of the automobile, her ferocious barking turned to joyful whelps as she raced alongside us. A sure sign that these two had brought good times and adventure with them.

"What's your dog's name?" the woman asked,

"Mollie," I answered. "Mollie Belle Morningstar, to be exact."

As we rounded the old oak tree and pulled up the dirt drive, I could see Mama hanging laundry on the line, pristine white sheets flapping around her. Her apron had pockets in front to hold wooden clothespins, so she wouldn't have to bend over to get more from the woven basket. Daddy had brought that basket home just last week, and Mama had chastised him for spending our cash.

Money. That was all Mama thought about anymore.

Daddy said it was because there was a lot of heartache going around, with people that didn't have enough, thanks to the drought and banking problems. Especially in the Great Plains states, where people's crops had dried to a crisp and all but blown away—dust storms carrying off precious topsoil to who knows where.

Things were particularly bad up in Oklahoma. In fact, some of my mother's people had come down from there just last week looking for work. Daddy didn't have any work to give, but he put them up in one of our four empty work cabins. Every day they went into town looking for work. Maybe they'd find it. I'd heard tell Dallas had a little more industry than other places.

I prayed my father wouldn't be mad that I brought this couple to stay in one of the other work cabins. I comforted myself that they would only be here for a short while—at least that's the impression they'd given me. Maybe they'd even pay Daddy for the cabin. They must have money, judging by their fine clothes and fancy automobile.

"Hey, Mama," I said. "These nice people need a place to stay for a day or two. I thought maybe they could use one of our worker cabins."

My mother's look was stern as she surveyed our visitors, but I pretended not to notice. She walked right past me and extended her hand to the man, who was climbing out of the car behind me. I could see

Daddy coming down from the house.

"Ma'am," the man named Bud said to my mother, "we sure could use some hospitality. We can pay cash for a room and something to eat."

My father's long-legged strides brought him up beside the strangers, and he answered for my mother. "We have an open cabin." He gestured to the side of the long dirt drive. "You can pull your automobile up to the front. Or you can leave it parked here. If it starts to rain hard, you might consider moving it up to the main road so you won't get stuck in the mud."

Tall and muscular, my father was a quiet man who didn't startle easily. It wasn't like him to rattle on. I wondered if he was shocked by the arrival of the visitors and had lost his wits, or if something else had occurred that I didn't know about. He certainly wasn't acting like himself.

"Gerald." My mother gently touched his arm. "Let's take a moment to introduce ourselves." Standing ramrod straight, she turned to the couple. "I'm Ruth Morningstar, and this is my husband Gerald. I suppose you've already met our daughter Margaret." Always proper, Mama knew exactly what to do in any social situation. Even though her wheat-colored hair was falling out of its up-do, she looked the perfect hostess.

The newcomer took my mother's extended hand again. "I'm Bud, and this is my wife Doreen." My father quietly shook Bud and Doreen's hands in turn.

"Well, now." My mother gestured to the small cabin. "Let's get you two settled in. I'll have Margaret bring you over some stew and bread for supper."

"We only have the one suitcase and a travel satchel." Bud pulled the case from the back of the automobile. "I can manage it all myself."

I looked over at Doreen, who looked sickly in the sunlight. And even though it was too warm for the light sweater she was wearing, I noticed she grasped it closed in front as if she were chilled to the bone. I called out as my father ushered them up the dirt drive to the cabin's door. "Should I bring some fresh sheets and blankets before I bring the stew?"

"No," Daddy said without turning around. "Your sister Samantha washed all the blankets last week to get ready for the workers' return. Everything should be clean and ready for our guests."

His words were kind, but his tone was strained. I blamed his uneasiness around strangers for his unusual behavior. After they entered the cabin, I turned to go up to our house. I could smell the stew simmering as I came in, but I knew it would be some time before it was ready to eat.

"Goodness grief," I said looking at the clock hanging on the wall. "It's almost four o'clock!"

Mother handed me a plate of sugar cookies. "Why don't you take these to our guests, to tide them over until dinner time. Tell them the stew will be ready in about an hour."

Once outside, the sweet smell of honeysuckle on a fence line near our kitchen door wafted toward me. A bee buzzed nearby, traveling among the blossoming vines. The new grass felt cool and springy beneath my bare feet, as I had rid myself of my shoes as soon as I got home from school. It was a glorious warm day, yet for some reason I felt a chill as I headed toward the workers' cabin.

Without knocking, I jerked the sturdy wooden door open and went inside with my plate full of cookies. As I whipped the linen tea towel off to present my gift, I noticed that everyone in the room was stone still.

"Stew will be ready in an hour," I chirped in my brightest voice. "Here are some just-baked cookies to tide you over until then."

"Thank you, Margaret." My father took the plate from me. "Now run on back up to the big house and help your mama."

I looked from my father to Doreen, who was lying on the bed with her head propped on the pillows. Her sweater hung on a nearby chair. A bright splotch of blood seeped through a cotton bandage under her sheer blouse. A shudder of fear rippled over me. No wonder she was so pale—she was wounded!

"What on earth?" I heard myself exclaim.

I looked back at the man named Bud and froze. He was holding a gun on my father.

My father spoke without emotion. "Please go back up to the big house with your mother. I'm going to fetch Dr. Lyles, to help our guest."

"No," the man said. "You're going to stay here. Your daughter will bring the doctor."

"Please," said my father. "Leave my daughter out of this."

"No sir, you can't be trusted. I know your type. You'll head straight to the police, tell them who we are . . . You fancy yourself a good citizen, a Bible-fearing man. Am I right Margaret? Does your father always do the right thing?"

I couldn't answer, my heart was pounding too hard. I could feel the blood rushing in my ears.

Then much to my surprise, Bud turned his gun toward me. "Run along now, Margaret." He said the words as if we'd known each other our whole lives. "Doreen needs you to get the doctor and bring him back to the cabin pronto. Don't stop to tell your mother what you're doing."

As I turned to open the door, the man redirected the gun back to my father. Daddy's face registered little emotion; he simply sat down in a chair near the end of the bed. Yes, my father was a good man, just as Bud had declared earlier. But he was also a brave man. And I knew I had to be brave, too.

As I moved toward the cabin door, my father called out in a soft tone. "Take Gil. He's the fastest of our horses. And"—he hesitated—"be certain to tell Dr. Lyles what he's getting himself into here."

"Shut up, old man! Your daughter didn't recognize us and the doctor won't either if you keep your trap shut."

"Tell Dr. Lyles, Margaret." My father's voice held a serious tone.

"Don't you say a thing, girl! Or your father won't live to see tomorrow."

Before I could get all the way through the door, the stranger grabbed my arm near the elbow and gave it a twist. "Do you understand me?"

"Yes." My voice quivered as his hold grew tighter. I tried to sound brave. "Just let my father go, I'll bring the doctor."

He let my arm fall. "Do as I say and your Pa will be waiting here when you get back."

The outlaw pointed the gun straight at my father's chest. "We'll be waiting right here. Won't we, Mr. Morningstar?"

MICK

Running to Dallas hadn't been so much of a conscious decision as it had been a natural choice. I loved music, and the chance to be near some of the best musicians in the world was just too much. My father would never understand, so I didn't tell him. Just hopped a passing train and rode through the night.

But now that I'd made it as far as Dr. Lyles's house just outside of Dallas, I was rethinking my hasty exit. I knew my mother would be worried half to death about me by now, and she already had so much stress in her life what with my little sister still recovering from polio. That's the real reason I agreed to let Dr. Lyles call my father to tell him I was safe, and that I'd decided to live with their family for a while.

I like the idea of living with the Lyles. The doctor's wife, Olivia, said if I liked music there was plenty at their church. She'd added that if I lived with them, she'd expect me to go with the family to church services every time the doors opened. Her terms for staying seemed simple enough. I'd figure out how to get out of the churchgoing after I settled into my life here.

Sitting at the kitchen table, eavesdropping on Dr. Lyles's phone conversation, I listened as he smoothed out the rift between my father and me that seemed to have been there since the day I was born. I swear, the doctor should've been a diplomat. My anger subsided. It occurred to me that my father and I were both right on certain issues, and that the blow-up between us two nights ago hadn't been all that bad.

Truly, there was healing magic in the doctor's words. He was a natural-born peacemaker. Perhaps his calming influence was the reason why I'd headed his way in the middle of the night, when I didn't know where else to turn. Though he was a close friend of my father, I knew he'd never turn me out. In fact, he didn't even question why I'd arrived on his doorstep.

Looking up, I gazed out the window at the serene farmland. In the distance, I could see a girl on a horse, headed our way. Dr. Lyles had his back to the window as he said his goodbye in the phone receiver, but his wife was fully aware of the rider's approach. She glided across the linoleum floor to pull back the lace curtains. Mentally, she seemed to be preparing for whatever news the girl on the horse would bring. I guess this was the way it was for doctor's families. Emergency situations bearing down on them at any given moment.

"Jerome," she called to her husband without turning then raised her voice an octave. "Jerome, Margaret's riding across the field like there's no tomorrow." The doctor automatically started to pack his medical bag. "I'll get your suit coat and hat," Olivia said as she assisted him.

To my surprise, the doctor addressed me. "Mick, I think everything's going to be all right between you and your father. Just remember, you two aren't enemies—you just have different priorities. He loves you very much. That's why he's going to let you stay here."

The way he said it made complete sense. I didn't try to engage him further.

Without being asked, Olivia took his wireframe eyeglasses to the sink and began to clean them. "I'll put some of these peanut butter and jelly sandwiches in your bag," she said as she dried his glasses on a clean tea towel. "Don't want your diabetes to start acting up because you're not eating on schedule."

Dr. Lyles moved to a tall wooden cabinet and got out two bottles of rubbing alcohol from the top shelf. As he bent to place them in his medical bag, I could see the gleaming barrel of a gun peeking out from where he had just removed the bottles. Deftly, he covered the weapon with a few rolls of cotton gauze before turning to give Olivia a quick kiss goodbye.

MARGARET

I spurred Gil to go faster now that we were out in the open land and Dr. Lyles's house was in sight. I was glad to see the doctor's work truck parked under the side portico. Two of his children played on the front lawn.

"Jenny Leigh," I cried as I reached hearing distance. "Is your father home? I need to talk with him."

The slender girl clutched her doll to her chest. "He's here." She ran to the screen door and called inside. "Father, come quick! Miss Margaret needs you."

To my surprise, a dark-haired boy with bluish-gray eyes stepped out of the door. His wavy hair lifted in the breeze as he moved to the end of the porch. He looked to be about my own age, maybe a year or two older. I was sure I'd never met him as he wasn't one of those people you'd easily forget. Certainly, he wasn't from around here. When the boy saw I was looking directly at him, he winked and flashed a flirtatious smile—a pirate's smile, if you will. I wasn't sure I'd really seen it, considering I was obviously having some sort of emergency situation.

Before I could react to the stranger, I heard Dr. Jerome Lyles's deep voice saying, "I'm coming. Let me get my medical bag and hat."

I surveyed the two little female faces looking up at me. The older sister that had spoken earlier watched me intently as she held the tiny hand of a much smaller girl behind her skirt. The boy with the dark, wavy hair was watching me as well. He certainly had a confident air about him.

Breaking the silence, Jenny Leigh spoke. "This here's the son of one of Pa's closest friends," the girl said. "His name is Mick McLaren. He's from Houston, down near the Gulf."

"It's very nice to meet you." I nodded in his direction before gazing back down at the two children. I suddenly developed a twisting knot in my stomach. I knew I was leading their father into trouble. It would be wrong not to tell him the two fugitives were holding my father hostage so that I would bring a doctor.

Why-oh-why hadn't I recognized Bud and Doreen earlier? I remembered I'd seen a newspaper clipping of the woman once. But she looked so different in person—smaller, frailer. Still, I should've realized it was her. But I wasn't expecting to encounter a notorious person on my walk home from school. Nothing bad ever happened in these parts.

Still, she'd called him by his well-known nickname "Bud" when we first met. Perhaps she didn't know he'd be asking to stay at our place. As lost in my thoughts as I was at that moment, I couldn't take my eyes off the little girls. Babies really.

"What is it, Margaret?" The harried doctor flew through the screen door holding his hat, coat, and medical bag. His chiseled face boasted high cheekbones and soft, dark eyes. Without a second's hesitation, he came up to the side of my horse and gently stroked the stallion's neck.

"There's a problem at our house. A lady's been shot in her upper arm, near her chest. She's lost a lot of blood and is possibly going into shock." I hesitated before continuing. Fear flickered behind the doctor's dark eyes as my words registered with him.

Glancing at the two little ones who still stood within hearing distance, I whispered, "There's a man with her. He's holding a gun on my father until I bring a doctor. I believe they might be the outlaws we've heard so much about lately."

Our eyes met once again. The flicker of fear had been replaced with the confidence of a man on a mission. I knew he had made the decision to not only save the woman's life, but my father's as well. I let go of the ragged breath I'd been holding.

"Girls," the doctor without looking back, "Go inside and tell your momma I might be a while. Possibly all night."

The girls did as they were told. Guilt plucked at my very core. Perhaps I shouldn't have asked their father for help. Perhaps I should've ridden straight to Sheriff Green.

The dark-haired boy still stood by the door. I felt certain he'd heard at least some of what I'd said in confidence to the doctor, but it couldn't be helped. Time was of the essence.

Dr. Lyles turned to me. "May I ride your horse? The trip will be a lot faster across the fields than taking the winding country road."

As I got down from my mount, the doctor turned his attention to the boy on his porch. "Mick, will you drive Miss Morningstar to her home in my truck. I'll meet the two of you there."

He turned the horse toward our farm and rode like the wind, his lean form and the horse's muscular body melding into one as they raced across the land. He'd be at our house in no time flat.

I'd heard through our small town's grapevine, Dr. Lyles had learned to ride from a physician he trained under in West Texas, a legendary Texas doctor named Jackson Roland who went by the nickname "Dr. Dean." Seems this man had mentored Dr. Lyles from a young age, and had taught him just about everything he knew. When the boy was old enough, he'd sent him to medical school. One couldn't help but admire Dr. Lyles's skill with the horse. I hoped I'd done the right thing bringing him to the wounded woman.

Staring at the black dirt on top of my bare feet, I heard the screen door open and slam behind me. I turned to see Dr. Lyles's wife in the doorway, a set of keys dangling from her extended hand. "Mick will drive you home," she said with a strained smile.

The boy stepped forward and took the keys from her. "May I take Dr Lyles's gun?" he asked.

She shook her head. "Carrying a firearm into a tense situation is just asking for trouble." It was at that moment I realized I'd been talking to the doctor near the open window of his kitchen. She must've been listening to what I told him. I didn't blame her for eavesdropping; she needed to know what was happening.

"Please." He gently took her arm. "I'm real good with a gun."

She must have relented because he walked back into the house and came out with a pistol. Turning to me, he said the most peculiar thing, "Margaret, let's go assist Dr. Lyles with his patient." I didn't know what to say, so I just took his extended arm and let him guide me to the passenger side of the truck.

The truck's interior was immaculate, not a scrap of paper or a bit of dust. Someone had polished all the controls until they gleamed. Looking at this boy who was barely older than me, I couldn't imagine he knew how to drive. But he seemed very proficient at it as he steered the rumbling automobile back down toward the dirt road.

As he carefully avoided any bumps in the truck's path, he asked, "Is your house the big white one just off the main road?"

I felt suddenly timid. "Yes." But I had to warn him, too. "Did you hear what I said to Dr. Lyles earlier?"

"I did." He spoke matter-of-factly.

"You can let me off near the front gate and turn around and go back to the Lyles' house. No one would blame you for doing the sane thing."

He rolled to a smooth stop in front of the row of work cabins and said, "Go on into the cabin and let them know I dropped you off." A shock of fear jolted through me as I realized he was going to go back. But I recovered quickly and opened the door to get out.

He reached over and caught me by the elbow—the same arm the outlaw had twisted earlier. I felt a sharp pain.

"I'm going to back out of the drive and park up the road." He pointed over his shoulder. "I'll sneak up on the west side of the cabin, by way of that thick stand of trees. Don't let on I'm outside. Just make an excuse to open the far side window, if it's not already open, so I can hear what's happening."

"Sure thing." My voice squeaked. "I can do that."

I closed the door and looked at him through the lowered window, mouthing a *thank you* before turning toward the first workhouse. Wooden legs carried me to the door, where I rapped softly. The door swung open, revealing a sight that would be forever ingrained in my memory.

Dr. Lyles was removing the bullet from the woman's arm. Blood flowed freely over the light-colored towels he'd placed underneath his makeshift surgical area. On the bedside table I saw ether and a man's handkerchief. The woman's face appeared pale and lifeless against the plush pillows. She looked as though she were being prepared for eternal rest.

Bud loomed behind Dr. Lyles. The doctor was certainly aware he was being held at gunpoint, but he didn't waver as he attempted to save the woman's life. My father quietly observed from the corner.

Dr. Lyles turned to him. "Gerald, would you come hold this gauze in place?" He acted as if he were asking Papa to pass the peas at the dinner table. In a split second my father was beside Dr. Lyles.

"Hold it like this," the doctor instructed while he started to wrap the bandage. Slowly, carefully, he wound the gauze around the woman's arm, making certain not to get it too tight.

"Margaret," Dr. Lyles called over his shoulder, "look in my medical bag and bring me the black leather pouch that holds my scissors.

After a few seconds of fumbling, I found what he wanted and approached the bedside where he worked. To my relief, I saw the woman's chest moving up and down—but just barely.

As I removed the scissors from their pouch, her eyelashes fluttered. She gently coughed. Color returned, first to her lips and then to her cheeks. It was like watching sleeping beauty come to life again after being kissed. Except, of course, one would be hard-pressed to imagine Bud as a prince. I had no doubts the rogue would shoot anyone who got in his way.

I noticed, then, the lace curtains billowing in the open window behind the gunmen. "May I open the window further to get more air flowing in here?"

Bud stepped aside and let me pass, but not for a second did he lower his gun. I guess that's how it was for a person who lived their life outside the law. They could never put their guard down, even for a second. I almost felt sorry for him.

Or, at least, I felt some pity for Doreen as I watched Dr. Lyles take her pulse. The doctor was absorbed in his work he didn't seem to notice the danger around him.

My father, of course, was stoic as always. I wish I could be so brave.

MICK

It didn't take me long after I parked the truck down the road to move back up along the treeline by the fence, sneaking through lush low-lying brush. There were a couple of cedar trees just behind the work cabin that provided perfect cover, but they were positioned too far from the window for me to hear the conversation inside.

I sidled up to the side of the cabin and positioned myself under the window. As I'd requested, Margaret had made sure it was open. Leaning against the whitewashed wood planks that covered the outer wall, I tried to make as little noise as possible. When I put my palm down to balance myself, the earth felt springy to the touch. Above, I heard a man talking.

"I'm mighty surprised to find a black doctor here," the outlaw said matter-of-factly.

"I need to wash up." I recognized Dr. Lyles's steady voice. He wasn't the least perturbed by the comment.

"I'll get a bucket of fresh water from the well," Margaret said.

The door squeaked open and closed again. Then an older man, who I assumed was Margaret's father said, "You're lucky Dr. Lyles was willing to save your friend, considering what it might do to his reputation. A lesser man might not have helped."

No one spoke for the next few minutes. A bee hummed, feasting on a rose bush. A bird chirped in the trees overhead, and the eternal rhythm of the cicadas filled the air. I hadn't felt this alive in a long, long time, and it scared me.

Creeping around the corner of the cabin, I watched Margaret at the well. Her movements were graceful, though she was more of a tomboy type than a fru-fru girl. The kind of girl my older brother André would call "spunky." She had outdoor, healthy good looks.

Margaret caught sight of me watching her. She startled but quickly recovered. I gave a slight wave and slipped back around the cabin's corner, positioning myself underneath the open window again and listening intently.

"I don't think the patient should travel for at least a week," I heard the doctor say.

"We need to get on the road right after we eat." Bud's voice sounded worn out. I could hear him pacing the floor in front of the window.

A woman's voice hollered on the other side of the cabin door. "Open up, I've brought stew and biscuits for your dinner." I heard the old door creak open. "Dr. Lyles." The woman sounded surprised. "I didn't know you were visiting. Let me go back up to the house for another dish."

"I don't need a bowl." The doctor called out to the porch: "Margaret, step on in here with that bucket of water! As soon as I clean my hands, I'll be on my way."

Bud's voice was hard again. "No one is leaving until I say so.

I heard Mrs. Morningstar gasp. "What's happening here? Why is Doreen bleeding?"

"Ma'am, please stop asking questions." To my surprise, Bud's voice came softer and more in control now. "Just pour me up a bowl of stew, and I'll have a couple biscuits to go for Doreen when she wakes up."

"I wouldn't move her." The doctor spoke as he splashed his hands in the water.

"It ain't your decision to make. Too many people in this here cabin could turn us in to the Sheriff, if we don't keep going."

"Then let me go with you," the doctor reasoned. "At least for the next twenty-four hours. You'll need someone to watch her while you drive, to help if the bleeding gets worse."

"You have a point," Bud said between mouthfuls. "I was thinking I needed to take someone to keep Mr. Morningstar here from blabbing after we're gone. But I wasn't thinking of taking you, doctor. I was thinking of taking Margaret here. No way would the Morningstars risk their dear daughter's life. Taking Margaret is my best insurance policy."

Mrs. Morningstar started to cry.

Margaret said, "don't worry, Mother. I can find my way back home after Miss Doreen is up and about." Margaret moved closer to the open window. "You do plan to let me go, don't you?"

"I haven't thought this through yet," Bud said as he continued to chew. "Right now, I need a drink. Doctor, give me that there bottle of whiskey you got in your bag."

"Go easy on it, son." The doctor's voice sounded far away. "Your girl's going to need it for pain when she starts coming 'round."

ANTONIA

When the phone rang earlier, I knew it would be news about our son Mick. He'd left two days ago, and he'd never been gone that long before without letting us know his whereabouts. But this time, his leaving felt different. The heated exchange between him and his father had almost come to blows.

I couldn't understand why Mick railed so hard against our life. He'd made it clear he wanted no part of his father's wealth. No, he wanted to ramble about the country, singing and playing the guitar.

Hiding outside my husband Lucky's office, I listened to his end of the phone conversation. Judging by the relieved tone in Lucky's voice, it was good news about our boy. A couple of phrases were said loud enough that I could piece together he was talking to our longtime family friend, Dr. Lyles. I heard Lucky murmur a "yes" and, "If that's what he wants." Then, abruptly, he hung up the phone.

I rushed into the room, unable to contain my excitement.

"Was that Dr. Lyles? Did Mick go to Dallas?"

"Yes," Lucky's face held a concerned look. "He's going to be staying with the doctor's family for a few weeks. With spring break around the corner, he won't miss much school."

"Was there something wrong that made you hang up so fast?"

"The doctor was needed for an emergency. I didn't want to detain him. He was kind enough to call and tell us our son is safe. We don't want to drag him any further into our problems."

Lucky was seated on a sofa, staring out the window at the landscaped grounds of our estate. He selected this room for his office because of the view, though he told everyone it was because it was the furthest from the kitchen noise. Whatever, it was a calming place to think things through.

I sat down on an ottoman near him. "Come," he patted the seat beside himself.

I rose and went to the velvet sofa. Lucky put his arm around me, squeezing me like he used to when we were younger.

"Now, wouldn't our lives be boring if we didn't have Mick to shake things up? André is a good boy, but you have to admit he's short on excitement."

"What are you saying?" Even though I'd left Italy twenty years ago, I still had occasional trouble keeping up with Lucky.

"Let's just say if I get a call from the police in the middle of the night, I never worry that André's in trouble."

"Of course not, silly. That would be Mick they're calling about."

Sighing heavily, Lucky rose and went to his desk. "I'm so relieved to know he's staying with the Lyles. Maybe the doctor will talk some sense into him."

I stood and looked out over the freshly mowed lawn. A rabbit nibbled in the flower beds. "I don't know, trouble seems to follow Mick. I won't rest easy until he's home."

MARGARET

My mother asked Bud if she could go get my shoes and a change of clothes from the big house. For a moment, I thought he was going to let her. Then he changed his mind. "Just give her your shoes, you look about the same size."

He paced near the open window. My mother crossed the small room of the workers' cabin and gently moved my father from the straight-back chair. Sitting down herself, she slowly removed her shoes, delaying my leaving as long as possible.

My stomach was a nervous mess. I almost jumped out of my skin when Dr. Lyles touched my shoulder and pointed to the table. "Margaret," he said, "hand me that basket your mother carried the biscuits and dishes in earlier. I want to put some bandages and ointment in it. You'll need to dress the patient's wound at least once a day for the next few days."

I brought the basket to him.

"Don't pull the bandages too tight." He said as he put the medicine, bandages, and a pair of scissors in the basket. "Watch for redness and infection."

My father calmly walked over, picked up my mother's shoes, and brought them to me. As I put them on, my mother took off her sweater. Lightweight and the color of butter, it was her favorite. She handed the sweater to my father, and he took it to where Dr. Lyles stood beside the basket. With a sideways glance, I saw Dr. Lyles's hand reach into his medical bag and deftly pull out a scalpel. He slipped it in between the folds of the sweater my father was positioning on top of the other items in the basket.

At the same moment, my mother clumsily knocked Bud's empty stew bowl off the table onto the wooden floor. It clattered at his feet and broke into three large pieces. Jumping back, he moved his hand down. For the first time since I'd entered the cabin, his gun wasn't trained on one of us.

I heard a rustle outside the window. A hand with a gun moved into view.

"Put your weapon down and your hands up."

Bud didn't turn to see who the deep male voice belonged to. "I know you ain't the police," he said calmly. "The police would've already shot me dead."

As Bud stooped to drop his gun on the floor, he turned and fired straight through the open window. Outside, the rose bush exploded in a mass of crimson blooms.

The door beside me whipped open, and Mick entered with his pistol trained on Bud. Bud turned his gun right back at the boy.

The two stood in a face-off. No one dared speak.

Then, Doreen surprised us all by sitting up and saying in a drowsy voice. "Bud, do you know who this boy is? He's the second son of oilman Lucky McLaren—one of the wealthiest men in Texas."

She propped herself up further in the bed and gave Mick a once over. This time, when she spoke, her voice was stronger. "I saw this boy and his family in the newspapers just the day before yesterday. I think his father may be running for governor."

2 BAD TIMES A-COMING

MICK

In order to keep Bud from hurting us all, I volunteered to go with him.

But, then Bud decided he still wanted to take Margaret. Looking back over my shoulder, I observed Margaret in the back seat, with Doreen's head nestled in her lap and her mother's basket on the floorboard.

"How you two doing back there?" Bud hollered into the wind rushing through the windows.

Doreen didn't answer. Margaret did. "I think we should stop somewhere with a bed. She's very pale. I could give her a biscuit and another shot of whiskey for her pain."

Bud considered Margaret's words before answering. "We've only been on the road an hour or so. Let's get a little further out, and I'll stop at a friend's place, see if he can hide us for a few days. He owes me a big favor."

No one said anything as we rode down the lonesome asphalt highway. Only one or two automobiles had passed us since we'd gotten on the road back in Dallas. At one point, we'd even seen a farmer driving a horse and wagon in front of us. Bud slowed to a crawl before passing it. In some ways, he was quite thoughtful. I wondered how he'd ended up where he was in life. My only thought was, something terrible must've happened in his past.

As the sun started to dip in the sky, scattering an array of purple clouds against a backdrop of golden pink, Bud put on the Ford's headlights. I wanted to ask Margaret if she thought the sunset pretty, but I didn't dare look back again.

* * *

After another couple hours, Bud exited the main road. In our dim headlights, I could just make out a road turning off from the byway we were traveling—really more of a dirt path, with high weeds growing on either side.

I expected Bud to drive right by it, but he whipped the car to the right and turned his spanking-new automobile down the old dirt road. His face winced with each shot his expensive tires took. I couldn't believe they were holding up under these conditions. We should have been on a buckboard, considering how many bumps and potholes we encountered.

Every once in a while, a moan escaped from Doreen's clamped lips. Couldn't Bud hear she was hurting and he needed to slow things down a bit? It seemed a shame we couldn't just take her to a hospital and get her proper care. But Bud said she was just as wanted by the law as he was, if not more so. I didn't ask for specifics because I felt I could piece the scenario together from the few things I'd read in the newspapers. Also I'd figured out by now that her name wasn't Doreen, but I didn't dare call her by her real name.

As if he read my mind, Bud asked, "What do they call you, boy?" He stared straight ahead.

"Mick," I said.

"Mick. We're going to introduce you as Sam Smith. The story is, we picked you up down San Antonio way. You've been riding with us for weeks." With that, he steered the car off the dirt road and down what amounted to little more than a path. "Don't you let none of these fine people know your real name. You hear me?"

I nodded affirmatively.

The lamps on the front of the car hardly put out enough light to see the path in front of us. Dark trees bowed overhead, their limbs cut back just enough to let us pass. Somewhere in the distance I heard a train whistle, which meant we couldn't be too far from civilization or our ticket out of here.

A dark figure emerged from the woods. I felt sure it was a wolf, but Bud assured me it was his friend's dog. "It might be a wolf," Doreen agreed from the backseat. "But don't tell Elvin—he considers it his pet."

The fierce dog ran like a shadow alongside our creeping ride, the animal's teeth gleaming in the lamplight. Never once did it bark. Perhaps that's the best kind of guard dog to have, one that can discern friend from foe with just a glance. I hoped his master would leash him up when he saw it was Bud and Doreen visiting.

But no such luck.

As we approached, Bud's friend came out on the porch with a shotgun. The dog went and settled at his side.

"Roll down your window," Bud said. I did as I was told. "Hey, Elvin! It's me Bud and I've got a couple friends with me. My lady's hurt, and we sure could use a place to stay for a few days."

Elvin just nodded and lowered his shotgun.

Bud rolled to a stop and put it in park, then slowly got out of the car. It could've been my imagination, but he seemed to be holding his hands up as if to indicate he came in peace. The menacing dog moved closer to its master and tapped its feet on the wooden porch boards. Still, it did not bark.

I watched the two men shake hands. Bud pointed back at us in the automobile. "That there is Sam and his friend Margie. You know Doreen."

Elvin was as silent as his dog.

"Sam," Bud called out. "Help Doreen out of the backseat. See if you can get her inside to the back bedroom. It's about time for Margie to change the dressing on her wound."

Margaret helped the pale Doreen sit upright in the backseat. Once she was certain Doreen was okay, Margaret slid out and calmly walked around to where I already had the back-passenger door open.

The frail woman wrapped one arm around my shoulder and the other around Margaret's. Cautiously, the three of us approached the steps. As we came closer, the dog's tail began to wag. He pranced near his owner, but didn't charge. He was well trained.

As we ascended the steps, Doreen let out a moan and transferred her weight to my side.

"Her arm is hurting her." Margaret shifted the basket of whiskey and medical supplies she was carrying. "I should probably give her a drink as soon as you get her up these stairs."

At the mention of stairs, a small shriek escaped from the woman. She fainted dead away. The canine whimpered in empathy.

"It's okay, Pearl," Elvin said as he bent to rub his dog's sleek fur.

"I know how you like Miss Doreen. We're going to get her back on her feet, aren't we?" Putting down his gun, he motioned toward the door. "Bring her right on in here to the third bedroom down the hall."

Suddenly neither Elvin nor his dog Pearl seemed threatening. I let out a sigh as Bud leaned in and picked up the petite woman I was carrying in one fell swoop. I could feel his love for her as he took Doreen from my aching arms. Clearly, the man hid a sensitive nature.

Standing to the side, I held the screen door open as Bud carried Doreen over the threshold. I gathered by the fluidity of his movement that he had the strength of an ox, deceptive given his lightweight frame.

Entering the house, I let the screen door shut with a soft thud behind us.

Warm lamplight showered the living room. In its glow, it was easy for me to see that Elvin wasn't some crazed villain. In fact, he had framed pictures of his kids and grandkids hung along the hallway. Margaret was right behind me as I followed Bud into the last room on the right. Turning to look at her, I noticed she was shaken. I gave her a pat on the shoulder. She hardly acknowledged me before setting down her basket of medical supplies.

Seconds later, she went to work taking care of Doreen. From the tender way she prepared to remove the bandages, I could tell she really cared about her patient. This Margaret was a special kind of person. I don't know if I'd be so kind if our places were changed.

"Mr. Elvin," she called over her shoulder loud enough for him to hear in the hallway. "I need some hot water in a bowl. Also, I'd like a clean towel and washrag if you have it. Nothing fancy, it'll probably get blood stains on it."

"Vergie," Elvin called out. "Can you come here a minute?"

From somewhere in the back of the house a woman's voice replied, "I heard her. I'm getting everything. Why don't you men go out on the front porch?"

As we hustled back down the hall, Margaret was already getting the bottle of whiskey out of her basket. "Take a little sip of this before we get started," she said to Doreen. "The dried blood has stuck the bandages to you."

Out on the porch, I sat in a decrepit straight-back chair. It wasn't dirty so much as warped through and through. Elvin and Bud sat in rockers. No one said anything. And no one turned on the porch light either. A bug buzzed by me and I reached out in the darkness to swat at it.

Elvin took out a pipe, and Bud reached into his jacket pocket for a Camel. He offered one to me, but I turned it down. Pearl came out of the shadows and walked up the porch steps before laying down at Elvin's feet.

"Howdy do, Pearl." The old man leaned down and gave the dog a treat from his shirt pocket. He turned to me. "Don't let her scare you, son. Only tough when she has to be."

I watched the old man pat his dog affectionately. Bud added, "Just like the rest of us."

MARGARET

Talk about being nervous as a long-tail cat near a rocking chair. I didn't know what to do with all my nervous energy. Vergie was doing a fine job of medicating and bandaging Doreen's wound. They really didn't need me.

I was amazed to discover how familiar the older woman was with dressing wounds. Like a nurse. I stood by and waited to help her in any way I could. My dress pocket held the scalpel Dr. Lyles had slipped into my basket back at the cabin. It might be small, but it was sharp, and it might just keep me and Mick alive. I didn't dare touch it, but I could feel its cold steel against my stomach.

"What do you think his life is like?" Doreen's slurred voice jolted me into the moment. She was drunk from the whiskey I'd been letting her sip for the last hour. I figured it was okay as long as it kept her pain down.

"Who are you talking about, Doreen?" I didn't expect a coherent answer.

"The boy from the wealthy oil family."

"I don't rightly know," I replied softly. Apparently, she didn't remember Bud's direct order not to tell anyone Mick McLaren's real identity. But she hadn't said his name out loud. And Bud wasn't likely to hear out on the porch. Besides, Vergie didn't seem like much of a talker. The tight line of her lips told me she was deep in concentration as she rewrapped Doreen's bandage. Every once in a while, her sparkling eyes held a hint of kindness, but other than that she was all business. It was possible she, too, was nervous about the situation we all found ourselves in on this balmy spring night.

After she finished her doctoring, Vergie moved the small metal fan closer to the bed, lining it up with the open window so it would blow cool air over Doreen's feverish body. I suggested I get more warm water to give our patient a sponge bath. In spite of the fact I was scared half to death—and hungry, and sleepy—I knew a bath would help Doreen tremendously.

"A sponge bath is a nice idea," Vergie said. "But cool water is what we need." She took up the bowl she'd been using. "I'll go get it."

Her slender figure slipped out of the room, her cotton dress swishing around her legs. Her sturdy black shoes didn't match the dress, but in these hard times people were more concerned with having a good sturdy pair of shoes than with being fashionable.

"You didn't answer me, Margaret." Doreen shaded her eyes against the lamplight with her good arm. "Can you imagine the parties he's attended . . . the nightlife . . . the travel. His mama's real pretty. I read she's Italian. His parents met in the Great War, when his daddy was a fighter pilot." Doreen settled into the soft mattress and closed her eyes. "Can you imagine?"

"No, I can't rightly stretch my imagination that far." But really, I could. I too had read about Mick's family. Everybody in the state of Texas knew everything there was to know about them. Heck, I could even name his siblings in order. André, his handsome older brother who helped run the family business, then Mick, then Katherine his younger sister who'd recently recovered from polio, and finally little Bobby, the baby who'd go into first grade soon. No wonder Bud had wanted Mick for insurance— he'd probably get a big ransom for him. And with me in the mix, there was no way Dr. Lyles or my parents were going to tell the law they'd been there.

But, I'd also read about the infamous duo that had abducted us. Mick and I weren't safe in Bud and Doreen's company. The country's newspapers had romanticized their crime sprees, and they seemed nice enough right now, but I couldn't forget they had a history of doing *really* bad things. No doubt, they'd shoot us if it meant saving their own hides, even for something as simple as saying their real names out loud.

Doreen had dozed off with her wireframe glasses on. Carefully, I took them off and put them on the bedside table. I hadn't realized she wore glasses until she had had Vergie get them out of her purse earlier. She looked like a real angel, resting on the crisp white pillow.

Outside, someone strummed a guitar and began to sing. The sound beckoned me to close my eyes and lean my head back against the big padded chair I was curled up in. The singer's haunting voice floated in with the night air. I couldn't tell if it was Bud or Mick singing. It wasn't Elvin.

Tears cascaded down my face, cleansing my fears away.

"Let the tears flow," Doreen whispered from her dream state.

I did.

ANTONIA

When the phone rang, I didn't want to answer. Something told me it was bad news about our son. But Lucky rushed past me and picked it up on the fifth ring. His face went ashen as he told the operator he would take the call. I could hear Dr. Lyles's deep baritone on the other end, but I couldn't make out his exact words. Lucky let him do the talking, until the end. Then he said, "Have they asked for a ransom?"

Through the receiver, I heard the doctor's answer. A simple no.

* * *

Later that night, Lucky and I sat at the kitchen table. There would be no sleep for us this night, though it was close to midnight. How strange it was to think of our son Mick and the young farm girl Margaret being held captive by those outlaws.

If we went to the police, the outlaws might kill our children. But how could we just sit and wait?

Lucky stared into space as if he might find answers there. His brow furrowed, and his usually bright blue eyes held a dull gray. I had not seen him this disconcerted since his father died.

Oh, God, I prayed. *Please don't let my son die!* Lucky looked over at me as if I'd spoken the words aloud.

"I knew I shouldn't have announced my run for Governor," he said. "It has brought even more attention to our family. If we hadn't had so many family photos in the newspapers lately, no one would have

known what Mick looked like. Now, I fear the whole state of Texas does."

MARGARET

The men came inside and left Mick alone on the porch with Pearl. I guess they figured he wouldn't run off into these thick woods on this dark night.

Pearl lay near his feet as he played a soft Spanish song. His deft fingers had become one with the old guitar.

"Where'd you get the guitar?" I asked through the screen door.

Mick didn't move a muscle, just continued to play. Pearl stood up and stared me down.

"Sit," Mick said. The dog sat. "Down." The dog reclined at his feet.

Now Mick answered my question. "Bud had it in his trunk. It's old, but it has a solid sound." He finished the song. "Come on out here with me and Pearl."

I opened the screen door a few inches. Pearl rolled over on her side and yawned. Stepping out, I almost tripped over a rug they'd put out for people to wipe their feet. Vergie's doing, I knew. In the short time I'd been around her, I had observed that she was a compulsive cleaner like my momma. Inside Vergie's house, everything had a place. I wondered about her husband's connection was with Bud.

I tried to think of something to say. "You play pretty."

"Thank you." His accent wasn't thick, but it was clear he was born in Texas—more West Texas, I would say. Of course, I'd read his family's oil company was based out of Houston. He must've been born in the West before moving down toward the Gulf. One day I'd be brave enough to ask

I could feel his eyes on me, but I couldn't see him very well. "How are you holding up?" There was real concern in his voice. He sat in the shadows; the glow from the door didn't reach far in the velvety night.

"I'm okay."

Mick carefully laid the beat-up guitar on a nearby table, then stood up from his rocking chair and came to sit by me on the porch steps. "We need to make a plan to stay together," he whispered. "That's how we're going to get out of this. We both need to be alert for the right time to run."

The nearness of him set my heart to beating wildly. I ducked my head to my chest. He mistook my actions for being upset.

"Now don't cry." He put his arm around my shoulders. "They've been nothing but nice to us so far."

Then I really did cry, but in a different way than I had earlier in Doreen's room. This time, hot angry tears tumbled down my cheeks. I wiped them away with the sleeve of Mama's butter-yellow sweater, then immediately stopped what I was doing. "I can't cry on this nice sweater," my voice croaked a little. "It's Mama's favorite. And I'm stretching out her best shoes. They'll be too big on her once I get them back."

Mick took inventory of my cramped shoes. "No need to worry, I imagine your Mama will buy herself a new pair. ."

"Are you kidding? There's no money for people to buy anything these days, much less new shoes."

I hadn't meant to raise my voice. But only a rich man would be so casual about basic needs with all that was going on in the world. Especially for the people of Oklahoma and Texas. Crops burning up, deadly dust storms blowing, animals and people starving. *Lawd! Mick must be living some kind of fairy tale to think my Mama could buy a pair of new shoes just because she wants them.*

He took his arm from my shoulders and moved away a little. Picking up a stick, he held it toward Pearl, and the dog came over and took it from him.

"You're good with animals," I said ,trying to make things right.

"I am. You are too. I saw how you handled your horse when you came to Dr. Lyles's house."

"I thought you were inside."

"Watched you through the window. Quite a sight, you flying across the field at breakneck speed. I could tell you weren't the kind of girl to back down from a fight."

I didn't answer. His words were true, I usually put on a brave front. But inside I was scared silly. Putting my face in my hands, I bent forward until my head touched my knees. Mama's sweater pushed up against my cheek. The faint scent of her perfumed soap wafted over me, and I felt a little better.

DR. JEROME LYLES

I looked across the room at my old friend Lucky McLaren. He seemed to be holding up better than his lovely-but-bone-tired wife Antonia. Her eyes were swollen from tears, and her brow creased from worry. My wife Olivia sat beside her, holding her hand.

"I can't believe they haven't called with a ransom," Olivia said to no one in particular. "What do they want if they don't want money?"

"I think they needed to ensure they'd have enough time to get far away before we called the police," Antonia replied. "However, two days have passed. Perhaps they are planning some kind of ransom scheme."

A shy voice came out of the hallway shadows. "A ransom for Mick, maybe. They could see we don't have much money." It was Margaret's mother Ruth speaking. I'd almost forgotten she had walked over earlier to sit with us. They didn't have a phone at their house, and she hoped to be here in the event the kidnappers called. She had been sitting at the kitchen table, but went out to the front porch when Antonia started to cry.

"Please, Ruth," I said. "Come sit with us. I can make you one of my famous sandwiches and iced tea to drink."

She drifted into the room and pulled a chair to the table, where she sat wringing her hands. She stared at the phone as if willing it to ring.

Lucky got up to help me with the food. Soon I'd have to go do my patient rounds, and I couldn't afford a drop in my blood sugar. Diabetes was a hard disease to master, but I'd done well so far with careful diet and exercise.

Looking through the window, I saw Margaret's father Gerald striding purposefully across the field. The sunlight outdoors made a stark contrast to the darkened interior of our kitchen, and it hurt my eyes to stare. Soon, I heard his raspy knock on the screen.

"Door's not latched," I called.

With one foot inside he said, "I think we need to call the law. My daughter's life is at stake, and we don't have the money for a ransom. Margaret is not the kind of girl that'll hold up well in the presence of a bunch of crooks." He let his eyes adjust to the darkened scene before him, then he stepped over to the telephone. "Doctor, may I use your phone to call the sheriff?"

Lucky put down the big knife he was using to slice the ham and wiped his hands with a cup towel.

"Don't call the authorities yet," he said.

"I won't have my child in harm's way." Gerald Morningstar's voice held fear and anger as he lifted the receiver. "We've waited long enough."

"Hear me out." Lucky reached to hang up the phone. Gerald pushed his hand back.

"Gerald . . ." Ruth's shy voice held a strength I'd never heard before. "Let him speak."

Gerald looked back at Ruth, then at Lucky. "Say what you've got to say," he said, "but make it fast. I don't think anything can change my mind."

Lucky took a step back and drew himself up to his full height. "My Uncle Robert has a private investigator he uses for special instances, like when a client doesn't pay. The investigator is a ruthless man, but he's smart and efficient. He's just the man to bring our children home."

"I don't have money for an investigator . . ."

"But we do." Antonia said in the take-charge voice I'd known for years. "Let us bring this man here."

"Bud said he'd hurt the kids if we turned him in," Ruth pleaded. "You know he meant it."

Gerald stood with the receiver in hand, contemplating the situation. From way across the room, I could hear the operator asking if he wanted to make a call. I didn't know what to say—I could understand both men's point of view. Finally, he hung it up and stepped back.

"Call the investigator," he said. "I'll give you what little money I can to help with the costs."

MICK

We spent the night in the living room, with Margaret sleeping on the couch and me on the floor beside her. I heard the rooster crow at sunrise, and our hosts were up and at 'em before I had a chance to get to my feet.

The house was small, and the walls paper-thin, so it was easy to hear the two of them talking. Vergie asked her husband Elvin if he'd gather enough eggs for her to make everyone breakfast.

"Let me get the coffee going first," he answered in a gruff tone.

I heard some shuffling around before Vergie spoke again. "Those two kids," she said. "They shouldn't be with Bud and Doreen. Especially the girl, she's a good one. What do you think her story is?" That's all I heard before their bedroom door opened and they both tiptoed out to the kitchen.

Sunlight poked through a crack in the living room drapes, beginning as a faint golden glow and growing brighter as the sun rose higher. Today was the day of our escape. I just felt it.

I wanted to wake Margaret and tell her, but she didn't open her eyes during all the commotion. Just kept on dreaming right through the chaos.

I took the opportunity to really study her face. She was pretty when she slept. None of the awkwardness and uncertainty I noticed in her waking moments. Margaret seemed the type of girl that didn't realize her own appeal, and that made her that much more attractive to me. Usually girls came after me—or should I say my daddy's money—in a very aggressive manner. But not this girl, she didn't do anything to get me to notice her. In fact, it seemed just the opposite like she was trying to avoid me at times. And I knew she wasn't shy. I knew she had spunk because I'd seen her ride her horse like she was flying when she came to get Dr. Lyles. I guess Vergie had it right when she said, "What's the girl's story?"

I thought back to when we were driving out of Dallas yesterday. Margaret's face seemed to waver between shock and interest as we passed the downtown buildings before getting out on the open highway. The pegasus that had just been built atop the Magnolia building particularly held attraction for her. She stared at the flying red horse as if it were a painting in a museum or something. If I had to guess, I'd bet she'd never been that far from home before.

Through the crack in the drapes, I made out the forms of Elvin and Pearl walking in the henhouse yard. He must've slipped out the kitchen door so he wouldn't wake us. He couldn't have been out there more than a few minutes, but he already had a basketful of eggs. I watched him stoop over to talk to Pearl before he came back inside.

"What are you looking at that's so interesting?" Margaret's sleepy voice jolted me back to our situation.

"Just watching the sun come up, thanking the Lord for another day." I smiled over my shoulder.

"Did you know the name of this town is Fate?" she said with a little yawn.

"How'd you know that?"

"I read it on a sign when we were coming in yesterday." She sat up on the couch and put on her mother's shoes. "I kid you not. It read 'Welcome to Fate, Texas,' and I thought, Lawd Margaret, what have you gotten yourself into this time."

I liked the way she said *Lawd*. Long and drawn out—the way only a true East Texan would say it. The thought tugged at my heart, reminding me how far I was from my own family down near Houston.

• • •

We hadn't been up long when Margaret went back to check on Doreen. The hiss of frying bacon filled the air. My stomach rumbled. I hadn't eaten since noon yesterday.

Margaret came out in the hallway with a bottle of whiskey in her right hand and clean bandages in her left.

"Isn't it too early for drinking?" I joked.

She didn't bother to give me a smirk. Instead she headed to the front door. "I need to get Doreen's traveling satchel. She wants to put on

58

fresh clothes and do up her face this morning."

Popping up off the couch, I maneuvered in front of Margaret. "I'll get it."

She thanked me with her eyes. "It's in the back. Hers is the one with the floral pattern."

When I opened the door, Pearl jumped from her prone position and growled. Not wanting to look like a sissy in front of Margaret, I slowly stepped out. "Pearl," I said. "It's me, Mick. Remember we met on the porch last night? I was playing the guitar. You seemed to like the song pretty well."

"She can't understand you," Margaret said from behind the safety of the screen door.

"I don't know," I said. "Looks like she's listening.

Pearl cocked her head to one side and raised her ears, coolly observing me. Venturing out onto the wooden planks of the porch, I said. "Good dog. Nice dog."

I couldn't determine whether she would let me pass, so I pushed my luck by slowly moving toward the steps. After a tense few seconds Pearl relaxed and laid down again, keeping one wary eye on me. When I reached the trunk of Bud's car, Pearl gave a little woof. She watched me closely as I got the satchel out. Truly, she was a good guard dog.

To my surprise, I saw Dr. Lyles gun that Bud had relieved me of earlier back at the cabin, nestled in the trunk. Cautiously I slipped it in my jacket pocket before stopping at the passenger side door. With a glance at Margaret, who was watching Pearl, I slipped the pistol under the seat.

Up the steps I went, slowing my pace as I passed by Pearl again. She made a low *grrr* but didn't move a muscle to chase after me. Without a doubt, she knew I knew that she was the big dog at this house. There was no need to make any further show of force.

In the doorway, Margaret gently touched my arm. "Doreen says we're leaving today. Right after lunch."

I nodded and headed down the hallway, leaving the satchel outside Doreen's door. Margaret picked it up and shuffled past me.

* * *

Thirty minutes later, both Doreen and Margaret came out of the room and joined the rest of us at the breakfast table. To my surprise, Margaret had on lipstick and powder. It looked good on her, though she seemed self-conscious about it. Every once in a while, she reached her hand up to touch her cheek. Doreen, on the other hand, was comfortable in her own skin. With her lightweight dress and her hair pulled back into a neat bun, she might be going to a church meeting instead of running from the law with her vigilante boyfriend.

Heck, I couldn't even tell she had a bullet wound in her arm, it was so well hidden.

3 CIRCUMSTANCE & SPECULATION

MARGARET

Holding her satchel open for her, I watched Doreen fill it back up with one hand. Her makeup lesson had been fun. She reminded me in some ways of my older sister, and it was hard to imagine her in a holdup.

Vergie came into the room. "Come hug me goodbye, cousin."

Doreen shook her head. "I'll hug you, but I won't say goodbye."

The older woman put her arms around Doreen, carefully so as not to hurt her. "I'll see you again." Doreen gave the woman a gentle squeeze. "I can never repay you."

"Shhh, now! We haven't done enough, considering what Bud did for Elvin." The woman released Doreen and took a step back. "Won't you stay here and recover? Let Bud go on without you?"

"No, it's too dangerous to be here too long."

Feeling awkward, I put the travel satchel's strap over my shoulder. "I'll take this out to the car."

"I'll go with you," Doreen said. "We should hit the road if we want to be in Arkansas by nightfall."

"Arkansas?" Vergie echoed.

"I shouldn't have said that. Don't want to put you in an awkward position if any law officers come nosing around."

Preparing to leave the room, I caught sight of my reflection in the vanity mirror and gave a little jump. I wasn't used to red lipstick. Shoot, I wasn't used to *any* lipstick.

Vergie read my mind: "It's amazing how a little paint and powder can transform a female." She gave me a hug, as she'd done earlier with Doreen. "You come back and visit too. I've enjoyed your company."

I doubted I would ever be back this way, but I nodded anyway. "Thank you, ma'am."

Outside, I looked up at the clear blue sky. This day was no different from a thousand other spring days in Texas, but my stomach wouldn't release its powerful knot. I'd secretly hoped Bud and Doreen would leave us here in Fate with Vergie and Elvin. But now we were on our way again.

* * *

Mick sat shotgun and I rode in back with Doreen. I positioned myself behind Bud, so I could use the scalpel Dr. Lyles had slipped to me earlier, if the occasion arose. I might be able to hold it to Bud's or Doreen's throats, but I doubted I'd have much of a chance against Bud's gun.

We drove in silence for thirty minutes or so, until Bud called back to Doreen: "You alright with the radio? We won't turn it on if it hurts your head or anything.

"I'd like to hear it," she replied. "I'm feeling fine this morning."

Mick reached over and the radio speakers crackled to life. The Carter Family was performing "Will the Circle Be Unbroken" but they were doing it a little differently than what I'd heard in the past. The chorus was changed up.

Much to my surprise, Doreen began to sing with the radio. She wasn't lying when she said she felt better. I'd taken her for almost dead this time yesterday, but the body's ability to heal itself is a mysterious thing.

She held her hair back from the wind coming through the windows. "Sing with me, Margaret."

So I did.

I sang loud and clear, just like she did, with none of the shyness I'd shown in the past when strangers asked to hear my voice. I hated to admit it, but it was fun, flying down the highway singing at the top of my

lungs. Up in the front passenger seat, Mick joined in. Then Bud. It isn't

often you get to sing hymns with outlaws.

If Doreen hadn't been watching me, I'd have pinched myself to

make sure I wasn't dreaming. But she was watching. When the song

ended, she said, "Goodness gracious! Where did you learn to sing like

that?"

"Your voice is pretty, too, ma'am." Bud said. "It sounded like a

chorus of angels back there."

"Thank you, dear." She patted his shoulder.

We drove in silence as the radio played an instrumental song.

After a while, Bud called out into the wind, "You people getting hungry?"

He hung his arm out the window as he drove. He seemed to enjoy the

thrill of being on the run.

"I am," Doreen called.

"How about that hamburger place just this side of Cooper?"

Mick said.

"Now boy, how do you know about that joint?" Bud looked

serious. "You from around here?"

"I'm from Houston," Mick said. "But I've traveled this way with

my Uncle Robert. We go all over Texas because of our family business,

and he knows the best places to eat."

Bud slowed the car a little and his happy-go-lucky attitude took a turn toward serious. Innately, we all knew better than to talk while Bud was thinking. No one uttered a word as we sped past fields of newly planted cotton. White puffy clouds pushed forward against a blue canvas of sky, and I tried to pick out animal shapes to pass the time. The high-noon sun's glare beat down on the highway in front of us.

"Hey, Bud," Doreen called out over the wind. "Do we need gas?"

Bud didn't answer. Instead he whipped into a gas station a little ways up ahead. I saw a sign in the window: "Pickled Pigs Feet Sold Here." I wanted to see what pickled pigs feet looked like, but I didn't dare ask to go inside.

After we rolled to a stop near the gas tank, Bud asked Mick to fill 'er up while he went inside and paid. I got out of the car to stretch my legs, and Doreen made a beeline for the ladies' room on the side of the station. It was unlocked and she didn't have to wait.

I went over to the gravel parking lot's edge. Just beyond the lot was a patch of weeds with a dandelion growing out of it, already turned to seed. I picked the delicate plant out of the weeds and looked at the white school house next door. I made a wish, then blew the little flower to smithereens. The cottony seeds caught in the breeze, floating up and away as they sent my wish to heaven.

Turning back toward the automobile, I watched Mick hang the

gas hose up on the tank before sauntering into the station to find Bud. I drew in my breath. I bet Bud didn't want anyone recognizing Mick, but it was too late to stop him now.

A bell rang at the school. I turned back to watch a tribe of children parade out into the schoolyard. Several teachers ushered them, telling them where to stand in front of a large, hand-painted school sign. A portly man came out too, with a camera held by a strap around his neck. One teacher was in charge of lining the kids by height, and she kept going up to the children and moving them around. Short ones in front. Tall ones in back. Occasionally she smoothed a cowlick or straightened a collar.

Behind her the man with the big stomach worked with his camera. For his size, he was graceful in the way he managed his equipment, though I doubted he was a professional photographer. Probably just the school principal. The thought crossed my mind that I might not be in our school picture this year, and I felt a heaviness deep in my chest. No documentation that I existed during my sophomore year.

Doreen gave a little laugh behind me, and I nearly jumped out of my skin "Oh, look at those children! Aren't they darling?" We took in the chaos unfolding before us. "Look Margaret." She produced a Camel from her purse and lit it. "Some of those kids don't have shoes on their feet."

I thought about telling her that's the way my classmates looked too, but I didn't. Instead I just stared at her perfect manicure as she held the cigarette so the wind wouldn't blow the smoke in my face. Deep inside, I knew she had been just as poor as me at some point, even though she affected a fashionable persona. No sir, I'd bet my last dollar fine things hadn't been a part of Doreen's life for very long.

As if in a nightmare, the youngsters in the schoolyard all started to scream at once. The whitewashed walls of the school stood out behind them as they scurried in a frenzied mass toward the door. Bringing my hand up to shade my view, I saw one young girl covering her mouth and pointing behind where we were standing.

Doreen and I spun around. Bud was coming out of the store, waving a bag in one hand and a gun in the other. Mick trailed behind him.

Much to my unbelieving eyes, Mick had a gun, too.

It was Dr. Lyles's gun. I remembered the doctor's wife's reluctance to let him take it.

Pop. Pop. Pop.

The flash of the camera made me turn around once again. The photographer was holding his camera to his face. Holding the camera high, he ducked behind a thick stand of bushes.

My mind whirled as I watched a teacher herd the last of the frightened children inside to safety. Her stricken face must have mirrored my own horror.

Whipping around, I found Mick and Bud holding their guns out at arms's length—pointing them at each other.

It was clear by the look in Mick's eyes that he intended to shoot Bud.

"If you're going to kill me," Bud said, "you'd better do it with the first bullet. I ain't afraid of dying, and I ain't afraid to kill you either."

Mick didn't waver, holding the gun level at Bud's chest.

Bud moved forward and so did Mick. The barrels of their guns almost touched.

At this moment, Doreen screamed. Not just your ordinary scared-woman scream, but a piercing shriek like a seagull over the ocean —only ten times more mournful.

Mick lost his concentration for a second. That was all it took for Bud to flip Mick over on his back, without even dropping his bag of stolen money. Suddenly, he was holding the bag and Mick's gun in one hand, while in his other hand he held his own gun. Poor Mick was sprawled in the gravel, staring helplessly at the double barrels aimed in his direction.

"Don't carry a gun, boy, if you're going to hesitate." Bud nudged Mick with his foot. "Hesitation will get you killed." He kicked a little harder this time. "Hear me, boy?"

My mouth, my legs, my arms were frozen. Beside me, Doreen

took a deep breath. "Whatcha gonna do, Bud?" She walked closer to them as I stepped back. Her voice was soft and low. "You don't want to go back inside over this boy, do you?"

Bud looked at Doreen for a moment, before turning back to Mick. "Get up!"

Mick got up.

Bud gestured with the barrel of his gun. "Walk out into that cotton field over yonder . . . just beyond the school."

Mick did as he was told.

Somehow, I found my voice. "Please don't kill him. Please don't."

"Margaret." Bud spoke like a parent admonishing a small child. "I want you to get your mother's butter-yellow sweater out of the back seat and go with Mick. The time has come for you two children to go home."

Was he really going to let us go? I wondered. *Or was he going to shoot us and leave us to die in the field?* Doreen took my hand and led me to the car.

"Keep walking, Mick," Bud yelled. "Margaret will catch up."

As she pushed the sweater into my quivering hands, Doreen tucked a small bag in between the folds. "Remember me, Margaret." She said softly "Tell me that when I'm gone, you'll remember something good about me."

"I will." My voice sounded like it came from outside of my head.

She gave me a slight hug and turned me in the direction of Mick.

I could see his lanky form in the distance, his dark hair blowing in the breeze. With hands up in the air, he took slow, measured steps over the clay earth as if to say to the world, *I'm not scared.*

He must've heard me running up behind him because he said, "It's okay. We'll follow the train tracks into town."

The squeal of tires on pavement was our only clue that Bud and Doreen were gone.

Mick put his hands down without looking back.

I turned and looked. I needed to assure myself we were really free.

A silence followed. I could hear my labored breathing inside my ears as I trotted along beside Mick's long strides. There'd be plenty of time to talk about what happened inside that gas station store later.

We continued our walk until we found the train tracks up ahead. When we reached them, we turned and started following them toward Cooper's downtown area in hopes of finding a train we could hop. As we came out of the plowed-up cotton field, the clods of clay earth that were so hard to walk on turned into flat grassland. It was a much smoother trek from this point; however, we still had to watch for large cracks in the earth. Spring showers had been scarce this year. Combined with the dry winter months, the earth had no other choice than to separate into large fissures—some so large I could put my whole foot inside.

As if that weren't bad enough, everywhere I looked I saw little mounds of dirt with holes in front of them. I hoped they were formed by crawdads and not snakes. *Margaret,* I thought, *You just lived through a robbery. You can face a few crawdads.*

Mick asked, "I bet your mama's too-small shoes are really hurting your feet now."

"This dirt is going to ruin them for sure."

Mick stopped and put his finger to his lips. I shut up and listened.

"You hear that?" he asked.

"Hear what?"

"Train's coming." He knelt and felt the ground. I did the same. The earth held a faint rumbling.

"You know what I'm thinking?" he said. "We ought to try to hop this train when it stops for water in town, and ride it all the way to Dallas."

He stood back up and started walking again, this time with purposeful strides. I rushed to keep up with him, trying not to stumble in a crack. "What if it doesn't go to Dallas?"

"The tracks go back to Dallas. I could see them all the way from Fate on our ride out here this morning. Dallas is a big city. It'll stop there. We can get off and call Dr. Lyles to come get us."

"Sounds like a plan to me."

"It's starting to slow down," he called back from over his

shoulder, "which means it's pulling in to its stop. We need to book it if we're going to catch the train."

He looked back at me.

"Can you take off your shoes and run? It's just a little ways ahead."

Hopping on one foot, I took off one shoe, then the other. My feet were red and raw. I had blisters on my big toes. I stretched them out over the dark earth. Hopping forward, I let a crop of dead grass pad my hurtin' soles for a moment.

Mick looked back again and said, "Ready?"

I nodded. "As I'll ever be."

We took off. At first, he left me far behind, but then he slowed to a trot. I was still a distance behind when he circled back and took my sweater and the little pouch Doreen had given me. "Watch out for those cracks in the earth up ahead," I huffed. "Some of them are so big, I swear if you fell in one you'd go straight to hell."

He laughed as he left me in his dust once again.

MICK

The water went inside the big engine and the train steamed and hissed. The squeal of the brakes hurt my ears as the big cars inched back and forth, improving their position. The open boxcar I found was rusty on the outside, but the inside was clean. A few barrels sat in the far corner. Other than that, the car looked empty.

I called back over my shoulder. "Might as well hitch a ride, instead of risking running into Bud and Doreen again."

In an effort to catch up with me, Margaret hopped across the blacktop road that ran along the tracks. She said, "Ouch, ouch, ouch," with each little jump. I felt sorry for her.

She stopped in a grassy patch and tried to put her shoes back on her swollen feet. She took them right off again. I got up in the train car and bent down, holding my hand out. In my other hand, I held her sweater and bag.

A bell started to clang, and a whistle drowned out whatever Margaret was saying to me. To my horror, the wheels clattered and began a slow roll.

"Get on now," I yelled, "or I'll leave you behind!"

I couldn't hear her response.

"Get on!" I extended my hand further down.

She caught it, and I used every muscle in my body to hoist her up.

I only got half of her body on the train—the other half dangled over the side.

I dropped the sweater and bag, then used both hands to drag her on board. One of her shoes flopped beneath the train wheels.

I had no choice but to jump down and get it. My side was killing me; I'd scraped it hard on the rough wooden floorboard while pulling her up. Now she was the one safe in the train, and I was running like a crazy man alongside it.

Wheel after wheel moved over the crushed shoe. I grabbed it and threw it back up to Margaret. She missed it, but I caught it on the way back down. I didn't risk throwing it again, instead, I blasted the shoe as hard as I could into the back of the train car.

I ran faster than I'd ever gone before and pulled myself up on the handrails of the ladder beside the sliding door, hanging on for dear life.

"Get back!" I flung my body around the door and inside the car.

Margaret didn't move fast enough, and I landed on top of her with a hard thud. I heard the breath go out of her. Rolling off as quickly as I could, I flipped on my back and looked straight up at the metal car's ceiling. Rays of sunlight glittered through the shafts in the roof. Margaret gasped. I gently turned her on her side so she could breathe easier.

She inhaled and slowly recovered.

"You going to be okay?" I asked cautiously.

She nodded affirmatively then coughed and curled up in a ball.

I stroked her hair. "I'm sorry I hit you when I swung inside."

She began breathing easier, so I shut up.

In the corner, I heard rustling behind the barrels. Margaret didn't look over. I figured she might be one of those females that got frantic around rodents. I'd take care of the situation later.

I noticed Margaret was careful not to make eye contact with me. Light from the open railcar door shone across her face. Particles of dust glittered in the shaft and made her look like a princess. I wanted to tell her, but I didn't want to sound like a chump.

Instead I said, "We'll be in Dallas around sundown."

She smiled, and our eyes connected this time.

I'm not a romantic type, but the moment was perfect. For the first time in my life, I thought I might find the kind of love my parents had. The kind of love where just being with the other person is enough to satisfy you.

Margaret touched my arm, pointing behind me.

Before I could even turn around, a deep voice said, "How do? Name's Cowboy Larson." I whipped my body around, ready to fight if needed. But there was no need. I saw only a regular guy like myself, tipping his straw cowboy hat with one hand while holding Margaret's torn-up shoe in the other. He had on the biggest belt buckle I'd ever seen.

He noticed me looking at it but didn't say anything, just smiled in Margaret's direction. "I've been rodeoing all my life, and I don't think I've ever taken a hit like the one you took today."

Margaret encouraged him by letting out a giggle. Cowboy Larson took a hesitant step closer, holding up the floppy piece of leather.

Margaret became crestfallen.

Cowboy put the shoe down near her. "When we stop in Dallas, I'll show you where you can get some new footwear." He took out a matchstick and promptly put it between his teeth. "I don't know where you folks are from, but you can't go barefoot downtown. I know it ain't summer yet, but you'll burn your feet on the concrete and brick streets. Besides, lots of restaurants and stores won't let you inside if you don't have shoes on. Believe me, I know."

He winked at Margaret, then took off his hat and smoothed his sandy brown hair.

"Spend a lot of time in downtown Dallas, do you?" I was trying to make conversation, but I was also trying to establish my territory with this character. I could tell Margaret was drawn to his peculiar ways.

"I have." Cowboy was still wary of me too. In spite of his friendly manner, I could tell he was whip-sharp when it came to making his way in the world. I didn't want to cross him if I could help it.

ANTONIA

I stood in the garden, looking over the latest rose blooms, when the rumbling hum of an engine joined in with the buzzing bees. Both sounds were soothing to me. Looking up, I searched for the aircraft. Soon, a speck came into view.

I sat down on a metal chair, leaned back, and closed my eyes. Sleep had evaded me since we'd come back from our trip to Dr. Lyles's house. I could do nothing more as we waited for word of Mick and Margaret.

It had been years since I'd experienced the kind of anxiety I felt this morning when our maid Harriet brought the newspaper from the porch. As Lucky spread it open on our breakfast table, he choked on his coffee. There, on the front page, was our son Mick.

To my horror, he was holding a gun alongside one of America's most wanted fugitives. Not for a second did I imagine he'd joined up with this notorious gangster, but I could tell my husband wasn't so certain. It led to one of the first true fights we'd ever had. I was sorry we'd turned on each other, but I wasn't ready to apologize. Lucky loved Mick in his own way, but I wanted him to have faith in him. The same kind of faith I did.

After discovering the photograph in the paper, Lucky went to his office. I don't usually eavesdrop, but I did this time.

He called the private investigator. The man did all the talking while Lucky listened. Finally, Lucky asked, "What do you mean, the man took more pictures?"

I strained to hear what the investigator was saying, but it was useless. So, I slipped out to the garden to clear my head for an hour. I was astonished when the maid brought me a message telling me Lucky had charted a plane and flown to Dallas. He'd taken his Uncle Robert with him.

* * *

"How are you holding up?" My eldest son André stood at the French doors that overlooked the rose garden. His dark eyes filled with sympathy; his brow furrowed. He didn't understand his younger brother any more than Lucky or I did, but he seemed to try more than the rest of us.

I held up the note in my hand. "Your father is going to look for Mick himself. He's chartered a plane."

"I know," André replied. "I wanted to go with him, but he took Uncle Robert instead. Said Robert was an expert at dealing with shady characters."

Lucky was right. When our oil company's reputation had been at risk some years back, just as the Teapot Dome Scandal was breaking, it was Robert's foresight that kept our business out of harm's way. Years earlier, he'd refused to do business with the guilty oilmen, despite pressure from executives at McLaren Oil. If anyone knew how to spot con artists, it was Robert.

I heard tell he'd inherited this ability from his father—a man people were afraid to cheat for fear of his retaliation. But would Robert's mental prowess be enough to save Mick?

MARGARET

Piecing together Mama's shoe was impossible. And, though I enjoyed going barefoot, I knew this guy named Cowboy was right. It would be too hot on the city sidewalks—and besides, it wasn't proper.

But I had no money for shoes. I would have to endure my bare feet until I could get to a safe place and call my family. Maybe a shopkeeper would take pity on us and let us make the phone call for free.

We'd be stopping in the town of Fate soon, one of the last stops before Dallas. I thought of the night we'd crossed through Fate with Doreen and Bud. I'd been scared silly. Couldn't even think straight. That seemed like years ago instead of days. I didn't even look like the same girl. I thought of the little pouch Doreen had given me. Even though I hadn't looked inside, I knew her powder and lipstick were in there because I could feel them moving around.

It took me a moment to get my footing in the swaying boxcar. Far ahead of us, the engineer let out a mournful whistle indicating the approach of a crossroads. That's what Cowboy had told us the whistle meant. He seemed to know a lot about trains.

"Might as well use the empty cars so they won't go to waste," he'd said. "Every other kid in the country seems to be doing it."

He assured me there were probably at least a dozen other stowaways hidden on the train. He cautioned us to beware of the railroad police. Said they'd kick us off if they caught us.

I found my mother's butter-yellow sweater in a heap where Mick had dropped it when we hopped the train. He was a good-looking boy, but he was a bit of a mess when it came to taking care of things. Probably used to maids picking up after him.

I was glad he didn't show any romantic interest in me. Though I found him attractive, I remembered what my older sister had told me about men: Don't pick one that makes you clean up after him. It's a sign they think their life is more important than yours.

The pouch from Doreen was still in the folds of my sweater. I took it out and folded the sweater neatly, setting it down on the dirty boxcar floor. Inside the little leather bag, I discovered not only a small box of powder and a lipstick as expected, but also a wad of bills.

We could eat something. And maybe, just maybe, I could get something to put on my feet.

"Mick!" I held up the cash. "Doreen put this in the makeup bag she gave me."

Mick's face showed true surprise. Cowboy's face did too.

"What you going to do with that cash?" Cowboy asked casually.

"Buy us all three dinner."

His face lit up. "Train stops for about twenty minutes in Fate."

"Then let's get it to go." Just then, the conductor started to slow the big engine. The metallic squealing of brakes sounded down the line. I stood, ready this time to jump off and take a risk. In case we didn't make it back onto the same boxcar, I tied the arms of my mother's sweater around my shoulders in a way I hoped was fashionable.

Slowly the train came to a crawl. Cowboy jumped down first, while the wheels were still turning. Mick followed right behind him. They turned and looked up at me. As I prepared to jump, the railcars heaved backward as the train moved into reverse. It didn't take me long to figure out I needed to get off before the train went faster.

I landed hard on the brick road.

Mick gently took me by the arm, helping me regain my footing. He led me toward Fate's town square, where a number of small shops lined the streets. Behind us, the railcars squeaked and squealed as the conductor positioned the big engine to take on water. A clanging bell kept time as the train rolled to a complete stop. It would be only a few seconds before I heard the powerful hiss of steam behind us.

* * *

My feet were feeling the afternoon heat as I tried to be casual about looking for a shoe shop. Fate was a prosperous town, and it had quite a few storefronts offering the latest fashions. Cowboy stopped in front of a booth that sold newspapers. The woman behind the small wooden newsstand also sold some kind of sausage, wrapped up in bread and pastries. The handwritten sign tacked up near her head read "Fresh Klobåsnik and Kolaches." If she'd spoken English I would have asked her, but it didn't appear she did. I watched from a few feet away as Cowboy bought one of the papers and three of the sausage and biscuit things. Before I could get my money out, he paid.

He leaned down and whispered in my ear, "Come with me, I need to show you something."

Puzzled, I followed Cowboy down the street and around the corner, leaving Mick to stare at a new automobile parked on the side of the bank building.

Cowboy's demeanor changed in a matter of seconds. As we made it round the corner, he held up the newspaper he'd just bought and stabbed his finger at the front page.

Nothing prepared me for the shock of seeing Mick and Bud captured for eternity in the black and white photo. Anyone who saw it would surmise they were two robbers making an escape.

Why hadn't the amateur photographer stuck around long enough to get the real picture—the one where Mick tried to stop Bud? Or the one where Bud had Mick on the ground with a gun to his head?

I couldn't blame the man with the camera for leaving, I suppose. It was a dangerous situation. Even I had thought Mick was helping Bud when they first blasted out of the station. Still, I thought I heard the camera continuing click behind me. Why didn't he share those photos with the newspaper?

Peeking around the corner, I saw Mick still admiring the automobile. I didn't know how to tell him. The air was hot and dry, making it hard to breathe. The sweater around my neck felt like an anchor, and I reached up to jerk it off. *Don't faint, Margaret. Just tell Cowboy the whole story.*

Even as I thought the words, I knew I wouldn't tell a soul. It would put my family and the Lyles in danger. Instead, I waved Mick over to where we stood.

"Did you know about this?" Cowboy asked before Mick arrived. "Because if you weren't a part of this—and you just met him—I'd suggest we lose him right now, while he's still checking out that bank over there. He's probably cooking up a plan to rob it right now. I want no part of it."

I didn't know for sure what had gone on inside the station during the hold-up. But in my heart, I felt certain Mick was trying to stop Bud—especially when he held the gun on him. Dear Lawd, if only the photographer had stayed around to take more photographs. Then Mick would be a hero, splashed across the front page.

Cowboy took my hand hustling me down the alley.

Mick trotted to catch up, calling out, "Y'all wait. We haven't gotten food yet."

Cowboy stopped and shoved the newspaper at Mick before pushing his straw cowboy hat back on his head. Anger flared in his eyes. "Take a look at this, pal!"

I backed up against the rough brick wall and waited for Mick to take it all in.

To my surprise, he showed no expression as he looked from me to Cowboy.

Cowboy broke the silence. "I'm no angel." He took his matchstick out of his mouth. "But this is where we part ways—and I'm taking Margaret with me. Not too many people in this world look like you, and this here photograph is plain as day. It's only a matter of time before someone turns you in."

My voice trembled. "It's not what it looks like." Hot tears flowed down my cheeks.

Cowboy gestured to Mick. "Take these biscuits and sausage, and get back on the train." He shoved the paper bag he'd been holding at Mick. "Me and Margaret are going to stay here in Fate. We'll catch the next train out."

Mick took the bag and handed the newspaper back to Cowboy. He turned to me. "I understand if you think it's too dangerous to travel with me. I wouldn't think less of you if you stayed here."

Cowboy had his hand in his pocket. The matchstick was back in his mouth. The sun glittered off his rodeo belt buckle. His concern for me was genuine, and I had no doubt he'd help me make it home. Besides, I didn't need anyone's help to purchase a bus ticket to Dallas. But I wasn't ready to leave Mick alone. He was on the run until he could prove himself innocent.

The train whistle sounded signaling its intent to depart. I pulled Mick toward the railcars.

"Mick McLaren." My voice came out a lot braver than I felt. "I won't leave you to go it alone."

We ran. The dread left me, and I began to feel a sense of exhilaration. We'd be home in a few hours. We'd get this all sorted out.

We ran across the blacktopped road to the train. With the black tar sticking to the soles of my feet, I felt like I was walking on coals.

So much for getting shoes. I jumped off the road and onto a grassy embankment by the tracks. Ahead of me, Mick flung his lean self into the boxcar. I couldn't be sure it was the same car we'd ridden earlier, but it didn't matter. I set my sights on the metal ladder that went up the side of the boxcar. I'd try Cowboy's suggestion of getting one handhold and then two before bringing my feet off the ground. That seemed safer than the way Mick got onboard.

Cowboy came running up behind us and followed Mick up into

the boxcar, pouncing and landing safely inside on all fours. I'd never seen anyone quite so lithe. Now it was my turn, and even through the train was barely moving, I blundered at my first try to grab the ladder. I jumped again. Again I failed.

"Give me your hand," Mick yelled over the clanging of the train.

I extended my hand as far as I could in his direction and felt him grab hold. Cowboy came up alongside him and grabbed my other hand. Together, they heaved me into the boxcar.

Sitting on the wooden floor, I fought to catch my breath. Cowboy watched me, with hand on hip. When he was certain I was going to be okay, he turned to Mick. "You didn't think I would let you go without hearing the story of why a guy from one of the wealthiest families in Texas would rob a filling station?"

I glanced in Mick's direction. There was no sign of emotion at having his face and family name tarnished in the newspaper—none at all.

DR. JEROME LYLES

I could feel my blood sugar dropping. If I didn't eat something soon, I'd start to shake. Inside my medical bag, I found a sandwich and an orange. What would I do without Olivia?

Soon, Lucky and Robert would arrive. I hoped the ancient airstrip just outside downtown would accommodate their plane. My friend had told me he could land anywhere there was enough flat space. Sitting here in the back of my truck peeling the succulent orange, I listened for the plane's whine. Only the hypnotic sound of buzzing bees greeted my ears. I loved living in the country. Total serenity.

I saw the speck in the sky before I heard it. As it approached, I stood up in the truck bed and watched. The plane circled overhead before coming down on the empty blacktop road beside the field. Genius—there was no need to take a chance on the rugged dirt airfield. I later found out it was Robert's idea to land there. I guess that's why he gets paid the big bucks, as they say.

Tomorrow Lucky and Robert would go to Cooper, Texas to talk with the man who took the photo of Mick and Bud. The investigator was headed that way even as they were flying here. I couldn't leave my patients, but I would offer them any assistance possible. When their plane came to a stop, I started up my truck's engine and headed their way. I doubt they'd seen the warehouse-type barn where most crop-dusters kept their planes for the short term. I'd point it out to them. Then we'd head home and I'd

turn in early. Mrs. Chaney was due to have her baby anytime now and I

figured it'd most likely come in the middle of the night.

MARGARET

"Hey, Margaret," Mick said to me as I gazed out at the passing fields through the open boxcar door. "What were you wishing for when you blew the dandelion in the schoolyard? You know, back at the gas station."

It was the first time he'd mentioned the gas station since the incident.

"I can't tell you, or it won't come true. Everybody knows that." I turned and looked at him but kept my voice low so Cowboy couldn't hear. "What do you want to know for?"

"I just don't know much about you."

"There's not much to tell. I've got an older sister and a younger brother. I'm not particularly bright, but I have a lot of common sense."

"Surely there's something you shine at?"

"I play the piano. And I sing."

"I heard you and Doreen singing in the car. You're very good."

I felt my face flush at his compliment.

Silence followed, with the only noise being the clacking of the train as it flew along the steel rails. I wondered how many other vagrants this train carried? Back in Fate, I'd seen at least five people jumping cars further down the line. I leaned back on my arms. The rhythm of the rails soothed me as we forged ahead. Never in my life would I have thought I'd be here at this moment, with these two people.

My thoughts wouldn't quiet down. Maybe, I considered, it would be best if we were caught and turned over to the law. Then we could tell the whole story. Except, I don't think folks would care for the fact that Dr. Lyles saved Doreen's life. They'd probably blackball him for helping a wanted felon. I knew he did it not only to save Doreen, but also to save me and my parents, but folks probably wouldn't care about that.

I wished Doreen hadn't mentioned they were headed to Arkansas. I didn't want to know any more about them. I felt a connection with Doreen, and it bothered me. I didn't hate her like everyone else did. I felt if people knew the true reasons she was on the run, they might be more sympathetic to her and Bud.

But that didn't account for the awful things they'd done—if they'd really done them. Mick had told me he didn't believe what folks said about them, considering they treated us so decent. There seemed to be no right answers. I wished my mind would quit thinking so hard.

Cowboy moved out of the shadows and looked down at where we were sitting. "Mick," he said. "You never told me the story of how you came to be on the run. I want the real scoop."

I too had wondered about this but didn't dare ask.

"It's not easy being from a wealthy family," Mick said. "People ignore me until they find out my last name. Then they shower me with attention. It's sickening."

Cowboy chewed on his matchstick. After a moment, he said. "Having money is better than being scrabble-ass poor. I've been in both situations, and I can tell you that's the truth." Cowboy's words rang true for me. Our family struggled. At times it bothered me so much I could hardly stand it.

Mick ran his fingers through his thick hair. I could tell he was contemplating telling us something else. We waited, as the train clattered through the night. "My dad thinks my brother André is the perfect son. Perfect grades in school. Always knows what to say at just the right time. I'm awkward at the galas and fancy dinners I attend."

He thought hard about what to say next.

"My father wants to groom me to run the family business with André, but I want to be a musician. I only get one life. We fight about it all the time." He paused. "I left so I could make my way in the world on my own terms."

Cowboy tipped his hat back. " Making music comes from a person's soul. You either have the music in you or you don't. It ain't nothing you can stop if that's what you're supposed to be doing. I'm sure your father thinks he's doing what's best for you. Seems like you two could work out some kind of compromise."

I'd been thinking the same, but Mick shook his head. "No, compromises." He was adamant. "I won't be happy until I've given music my all."

"Well, then," Cowboy said, "you should know I sing and play the guitar. And I'm good. Real good." He said the words matter-of-factly, with no trace of pride in his voice. He pulled the matchstick out of his mouth and pointed at us. "That's why I'm headed to Dallas. It's where lots of musicians get their start these days."

"Maybe we can play some songs sometime," said Mick. "That is, if you still aren't worried about what you saw in the paper."

Cowboy took a step back into the shadows. "We'll see how everything shakes out. Those dang newspapers are going to be on every street corner. You gonna have to watch your hide from the moment you get off this here train." He pulled the sliding door open a little more so we got a view of the sun setting low against the big city's skyline. Spectacular rays of gold and pink shot between the tall structures.

Mick held to the side of the steel doorframe. "Thank goodness its sundown," he said. "It'll be easier to hide." His words brought a chill down my spine, even as the warm air rushed over my face.

4 RED-BLOODED ADVENTURE

MICK

The ticking of the wall clock kept me company. I couldn't believe I sent Margaret away, but it was too dangerous for her to stay with me. After all, no one had seen her face on the front page of the newspapers. No one except Cowboy even knew we were traveling together. I trusted him to keep her safe as they went to find a phone and call Dr. Lyles. He could come get her in his truck and take her to her family. It was too late for her father to come with the horse and buggy.

Sleeping on a church pew was rough, but with its thin cushion of red velvet it beat the floor. The back of the next pew in front of me had wooden tray pockets holding hymnals. Someone had put a wad of pink gum on the corner of the wooden tray. A rebellious youth like myself, no doubt. The thought brought a smile to my face. This is exactly what my dad would say if he saw the vandalism.

Sleep would not come, but I was safe for the time being.

After the filling station holdup, Margaret told me that the cameraman had taken photos of Bud holding me at gunpoint. I wondered why he hadn't sold those photographs to the paper. Probably because they didn't tell as sensational a story as me and Bud running out waving guns.

I glanced down the church pew to where I'd stowed Cowboy's straw hat—upside down, to keep the brim in good shape. The fact that he'd given me his hat to hide my identity—instead of turning me in on the spot—said a lot about his judgment. I think Margaret vouching for me had a lot to do with it.

Listening to the clock and the occasional sound of an auto going by outside made me antsy. The only light came from a dim street lamp a block away. Never in my life had I felt so alone. Fear rose inside of me; I took deep breaths to fight it back down. Only Bud, myself and the old man he'd robbed knew what really happened inside that gas station.

I wrapped my arms around myself to keep from falling off the pew. *Oh God,* I prayed, *please help me get out of this mess alive.*

Footsteps rang hollow on the polished church floor. Another set of steps joined in unison with the first. I willed myself to be still.

A voice called out.

"It's me, Margaret."

I unfurled my arms and fell off the pew, onto the floor.

"Margaret!" I shouted. "Why didn't you go home like I asked you?"

I heard her start to cry.

"Don't be mad at her." It was Cowboy's voice

"I'm not mad." I made an effort to sound less upset. "It's just, you two scared me to death." I had yelled in anger, like my father did when something scared him. I didn't like myself for it. "Margaret." I softened my voice. "I'm glad to see you and Cowboy, but why didn't you go home? Your family is waiting for you."

I stood up. Cowboy didn't startle. He stood ramrod straight. "We called the doctor. Seems he was on his way to deliver a baby. Margaret told him you were hiding here, and he said for her to stay here too and he'd pick you both up in the morning." I noticed he wasn't chewing on the end of a matchstick for once. "Said if he was still delivering the baby in the mornin', he'd call someone at the church to take you both to Margaret's house. But he'd like to involve as few people as possible."

I looked down at Margaret's feet. She had new shoes.

DR. JEROME LYLES

It had been six hours since her labor started. Her husband Ruben Chaney—Rube, as most of us called him—was not holding up as well as Mrs. Chaney. Rube's only job was to make sure their other five children were asleep. So far, only the two toddlers were snoozing—and they weren't in their beds. They slept instead on the floor in the den. At least he'd given them pillows, and one of the older children had thought to put a blanket over the sleeping boys.

The door to the master bedroom was open. If I craned my neck, I could see Rube pacing and wringing his hands. The three older children played some kind of card game, hopefully not poker. Rube would never notice that's for certain.

When I took a break to eat a late dinner, I asked if they shouldn't be in bed. "No sir," Rickey, the eldest boy answered. "We're staying awake to greet our new brother or sister. We'll stay up all night if need be."

Rickey was a robust boy with bright eyes. In spite of his large size, he felt no need to bully his younger siblings. But they all understood who was at the top of the pecking order. His word was law among the young ones.

I asked Mrs. Chaney how she was holding up. I'd delivered many babies in my life, and one thing was for certain. Each one came into the world at the exact moment they were supposed to, and not a moment before. I felt no need to rush things.

"Judging by how the pain's progressing," she said, "I should deliver this young one by morning."

Her statement struck me as odd. As a doctor I'd noticed if people were going to die they often did it just before dawn. Perhaps this was also true for giving birth. I'd have to give it more thought at another time. Right now, I needed to concentrate on the situation at hand.

I was bone-tired. Still, I listened to everything this woman said about how she was feeling. Through the years, I'd discovered women have a sense about what's going on with their bodies—especially when it comes to birthing a baby.

* * *

Just before sunup, the baby decided it was time. I'd been napping intermittently when Mrs. Chaney called my name, and I ran to her and was surprised to see the baby crowning. It had only been ten minutes since I'd checked on her.

In the den, I heard Rube and Rickey arguing about whether to wake the two older girls, who slept beside the toddlers on the floor.

"Rube," I called. "Please come assist me."

He padded across the hardwood kitchen floor in his bare feet. When he appeared at my side, I smelled his bad morning breath. "Hold your wife's hand as we start the final push," I instructed. He did as he was told, and the baby we'd waited for all night slipped into the world, letting out a tiny cry.

I held her up for him to see.

Rube's face held a befuddled expression as he gazed upon his offspring. "I'm going to be sick!" he cried. Then he fainted straight away.

I hadn't realized Rickey was standing right behind him. He rushed to catch his father before he hit the floor, and I was so startled I almost dropped the howling newborn.

"Honey!" Mrs. Chaney held out her hand toward her unconscious husband.

"Don't worry, Mama," Rickey said over the infant's cry. "I've got him." He stretched his thin father along the empty side of the bed near his mother.

"Rickey, did you witness the delivery of the baby?" The concern in my voice was evident.

"Yes, sir," he said. "I'm going to be a doctor just like you." He patted his rousing father on the arm. "Guts and gore don't bother me."

I nodded my head affirmatively, recalling my days as a young intern following Dr. Dean on his rounds. Guts and gore didn't bother me either.

The baby's cry settled into a soft whimper. I wrapped the

newborn in a waiting towel, checked her over from head to toe, and cut the cord. Behind me, Rickey said, "I have the perfect name for my new sister."

My muscles tensed as I contemplated the names Rickey might come up with. A moment later, the rough and tumble boy blurted, "We ought to name her Dawn. Do you like it, Mama?"

I relaxed at the suggestion. I'm sure his mother did, too.

MARGARET

All three of us spread out inside the chapel, claiming our territory for sleeping. I selected the carpeted area up near the preacher's podium, using mama's yellow sweater as a makeshift pillow. Despite everything I'd been through in the last few days, it still held the faint hint of her perfumed soap. The scent brought tears to my eyes. Here we were so close, and yet I had to wait another day to get home.

I hoped the baby Dr. Lyles was delivering would be okay. It sure was taking its time. I knew if I was a baby angel, I'd be hard-pressed to come into this mess of a world.

Daddy said he'd heard through his cousin Delmar up in Durant that things in Oklahoma were much worse there than in Dallas. Just a few years ago Delmar had been bringing in a fortune, planting and harvesting wheat. But now the land had dried up, and dust storms were wreaking havoc up there. I told Daddy I sure was glad we didn't have to deal with their adversity. He replied, "Margaret, it's easy to avoid getting involved in other people's problems when they don't affect you." I told him, I guess that's the way of the world. If we got upset over everything worth getting upset over, we'd never be happy at all. Daddy looked at me strange when I said it. I guess there are no easy answers in life.

The church carpet underneath me was new, and the coarse fibers scratched everywhere they touched my bare skin. It crossed my mind that I could go stretch out on a pew like Mick and Cowboy. It seemed to be working particularly well for Mick, judging by the gentle snores coming from his direction.

Once in a while, I heard Cowboy cough deeply from his chest. Earlier, when I'd told him he might be getting sick, he just said it was residual dust in his lungs from the dirt storms he'd grown up with in Guymon, Oklahoma. I guess Cowboy probably had some sad tales too, just like cousin Delmar. If the time were right, I'd ask him. He did hint that part of the reason he was on the road was because his father's farm had failed, and he was trying to make music so he could send money back home. I didn't want to pry. But by the way my dad talked about helping people, maybe I should try to get Cowboy to open up. Surely it'd make him feel better to talk about it. There was no time like the present.

"Cowboy," I whispered. "Are you awake?"

"Shhh!" He made the sound so low I could hardly hear it. "Someone's outside the door."

I raised to a sitting position and scooted behind the oak podium. Sure enough, the door knob was rattling.

Mick stopped snoring. The door creaked open, and the lights in the outer hallway flipped on.

"Mick McLaren," a woman called out, not unlike a stern teacher about to discipline a student. "Mick," she called again. "Are you in here? Dr. Lyles has sent me to help you."

The light in the middle of the chapel began to glow. Mick raised up. His hair was sticking out at all angles and he smoothed it down with his hand before rubbing his eyes.

"I'm Mick McLaren," he said.

The demure older woman approached him with an outstretched hand. "And I'm Bertha Sinclair."

Mick went to meet her in the aisle.

"Doctor called me just before sunup and asked me to come help you and your friends this morning. Are they here too?"

I peeped around the podium to see Cowboy raise up from his pew. For some reason, I felt the need to remain hidden. Not that I was afraid of the woman, she was as prim and proper as you would expect from a church lady, and her soft eyes held a kindness. They actually twinkled when she spoke to Mick.

"Margaret," Mick said without looking in my direction. "Margaret, Missus Sinclair has come to take you to your parents' house."

Bertha Sinclair scanned the room. "Where you at, honey?" For some reason, I remained frozen.

"Come on out." Mick still wasn't looking in my direction. "Don't you want to go home?"

My feet hurt. My stomach growled with hunger, and my left foot was asleep from laying on it wrong

Bertha looked over the room one more time before saying, "I don't have an automobile so I can't get you home just yet. However, I can hide you pretty well in the music room." Looking straight at Mick, she continued, "Dr. Lyles explained the situation you're in to me."

Cowboy walked over to Mick and Bertha. I remained hidden.

"Please, come with me." Bertha motioned them down the aisle and out into the hallway. Turning back, she said to me, "Margaret, you're welcome to stay behind the podium. If you need us, we'll be downstairs. First door on the left."

She reached up and shut off all the lights. I could see the first rays of dawn coming through the stained-glass window. I tell you, even though it wasn't that scary, I felt the need to join them. I grabbed my sweater and headed down the aisle. Not even the pins and needle tingling in my leg could stop me now.

Jerking through the doorway into the hall, I called, "Wait for me."

I could hear them on the staircase. Mick emerged at the bottom and waited. For some strange reason, tears had started to leak out of my eyes when they left me in the chapel. Now they were flowing over my cheeks.

"Hey, it's going to be okay." He wrapped me in a loving embrace.

"I was coming back to get you. I wasn't going to leave you alone."

I could feel the vibration of his heart on the side of my face. The tears still flowed.

"Shhh, shhh." He wiped my tears away. "What is it? What's wrong?"

"I don't know," I said. "I can't stop crying."

"Me neither." To my surprise, his eyes were glistening too. He tried to smile as he took his arm from around me and wiped his brimming teardrops. "We're safe now, Margaret," he said pulling me close again.

MICK

The music room consisted of a few wooden bleachers for choir practice and an odd assortment of musical instruments, including a cello, a guitar and an upright piano. Choir robes hung on hooks in a row on one wall. I'd never been back here, although I was pretty sure Doctor Lyles's wife Olivia had spent a great deal of time practicing with the church choir in this very room. She was always talking about music and choral practice. In fact, her gospel music was a big draw for getting me to come to church with her and the family.

Standing in the middle of the room, I looked around at the plain practice area.

Cowboy went to pick up the guitar. Let me tell you, he wasn't joking back in the boxcar when he said he could play. His fingers flew like greased lightning. A brief wave of jealousy rolled through me as I listened. My own playing was not in his league. But, then again, I'd come to Dallas to learn to play like that.

The door behind me burst open and a big black lady rushed into the room. I recognized her from my visit a year ago. She wasn't much older than me, maybe nineteen or twenty, but she filled the room with her presence.

"Now that's what I call making a joyful noise unto the Lord!" She approached Cowboy with a big smile on her pretty face. "Boy, where did you learn to play like that? You go any faster, you'll set your guitar on fire."

She had come to sing on a spiritual tour when I was up here in Dallas. She'd played a guitar just as good as any man—even better. And, her music was unlike any I'd heard before—a soaring blues mixed with swinging soul. She held me spellbound with her unique style of singing and stomping. The crowd had kept time clapping to her spirituals. I was truly moved by her performance.

"Sister Rosetta," Bertha Sinclair said with a smile. "This here is Cowboy and his two friends." She sheepishly added, "I'd forgotten you were sleeping in the sanctuary guest quarters. I hope we didn't wake you."

"You did wake me." The woman's husky voice filled the practice room. "But I've always got time for fellow musicians. Are you three doing the church circuit like me?"

"No, ma'am," Cowboy said. "Missus Sinclair's just helping us out of a tough spot. I usually play in clubs and bars."

"Me too," said Sister Rosetta. "Sometimes it causes a stir among the church goers, doesn't it Bertha?"

Bertha nodded. "But the pastor says you're bringing God's word to the people who need it most.

"Amen, Sister!" A fresh-faced black man stepped in behind Sister

Rosetta. "Hello, everyone, I'm Thomas, Rosetta's husband. I'm along on tour too, but I don't sing. I preach." He said with a beaming smile.

"Rosetta," said Bertha.

"Yes," she answered.

"You met Dr. Lyles on your last visit."

"Yes," Rosetta and Thomas both chimed together.

"Well, this is his neighbor, Margaret. Dr. Lyles is out delivering a baby and he called me before sunup and told me to try to find Margaret a way home. This boy Mick needs to go with her. He's staying at the Lyles place."

"We can take you there now, can't we Thomas? Just let us get dressed properly."

Rosetta started to sing out praises to the Lord as she danced out of the room. Thomas followed her, clapping in time.

And just like that we were on our way home.

My head was reeling from talking to Sister Rosetta. Ever since I'd seen her play last year, she's profoundly influenced my musical style. What she was bringing to the world of music was unlike any musician before her, and I intended to be part of it. All in all, I thought, it was a much better start to the day than I'd anticipated.

Immediately after Rosetta and Thomas exited the room, Cowboy walked over to me with his guitar still in hand. "What was that?"

"A musical miracle, my friend. And if you think she can sing, wait till you hear her play the guitar."

* * *

The wind whipped Margaret's long hair into my face. She tried to hold it down, but it was no use.

Thomas was driving pretty fast in his new Packard touring car, shiny red with a white top. Heads turned as we rolled through downtown Dallas. I was enjoying the drive, even though I was stuck in the middle of the backseat between Margaret and Cowboy.

"Sugar," Rosetta turned from the passenger seat and addressed me. "Sister Bertha told me all about what happened to you and Margaret, and about you making front page news." She paused. "Thomas and I were thinking maybe you should go hang out with some friends of ours in Dalhart, up near the border, until you can get everything right with the law." She maneuvered in the seat. "Cowboy, they can use a good guitarist at one of the local bars out there if you want to go with him."

"Thank you, ma'am," Cowboy said. "Got to get myself a guitar before I can take the job, but I've got money saved to buy one if you know of anyone selling."

Thomas called back to us from the driver's seat. "Brother Joe has a sweet-sounding guitar he's looking to sell."

"Yes, he does." Sister Rosetta said. "I tell you what, you two kids come to Deep Ellum tomorrow night to see me play. I'll make sure Joe brings his guitar, and I'll get you the address in Dalhart." The scarf around her neck blew in the wind, and hit me in the face. She laughed as she pulled it back. "Mick, Margaret and I are going to beat you silly before you get out of this car. Aren't we Margaret?" She threw back her head and laughed.

I thought about telling her that Cowboy and I weren't kids, that we were probably close to her in age. But I decided against it because she was clearly significantly advanced beyond us, both musically and in the ways of the world. Instead I mumbled something about wanting to be a musician too.

"Can you play like this 'un here?" she asked.

I looked over at Cowboy, who was blushing with pride while holding his white straw hat.

"No, ma'am, I'm not that good," I said.

She smiled at me from the front seat.

"That's the wrong answer Mick. You're supposed to say, 'No, ma'am, I'm not that good yet.' And say it with confidence. Because if you can't see yourself doing it, ain't nobody else going to see you doing it neither. You know what I mean?"

I looked over at Margaret, who was still holding her hair to keep from whipping me with it. She stared up at Sister Rosetta, hanging on her every word. Clearly the lady was making an impact.

MARGARET

As we approached my parents' house, I started to get misty eyed. I missed them so. But I was also going to miss Mick and our long talks. He thought I was special, and I liked seeing myself through his eyes. It gave me new confidence. However, the end of the road was near. I couldn't go with him to Dalhart; I could only hope he'd keep in contact with me through letters and phone calls once he'd gotten all this behind him.

Mick gave me a nudge. Thomas was saying something.

"Is this your drive up ahead?" Thomas repeated himself.

"Yessir, turn left at the big oak. That's our dog, Mollie Belle, running to meet us. She'll get close to your wheels when she barks, but she doesn't mean any harm."

Thomas gave a short laugh before slowing his car to a crawl. He turned into the gravel drive just as Mollie Belle came up on the passenger side. When she saw me inside, her warning bark became almost gleeful. I couldn't wait to get out. Mick had been holding my hand, and when I jumped out of the automobile he got out behind me.

"I'll just be a minute," he said to the others. "I want to say goodbye."

He grabbed my hand again and continued to hold it as we walked toward the side kitchen door of the house.

Mollie Belle jumped all around us and I tried to pet her with my free hand.

"Margaret," Mick's voice was serious. "I'm going to miss you. I know we've only known each other a short time, but I reckon we're further down the road than just getting to know each other. What I'm really trying to say is maybe when I get things right, I'd like to ask you on a proper date?"

"But you live so far away . . ."

"No, I've decided to stay in Dallas."

With that the side door opened and my father came out.

"I'll be back, Margaret," Mick whispered quickly.

Daddy's arms opened wide to hug me close. In the background, I heard Sister Rosetta say, "Baby girl, don't it feel good to be home?"

"Yes." I was crying now. "Yes."

I looked up to see my mother and sister running from the chicken coup, and my brother emerging from the barn as if he'd heard the dinner bell. Running like a maniac, he passed the others on the dirt path. Mollie Belle barked as if to say, "Look who's home!"

My father hugged me tighter. "Are you okay? Please tell me you're okay."

"I'm good, Daddy."

Looking up at my father, I saw him turn to face Mick. I could see emotion on his weathered face, the face of a man who'd tried to do the right thing his whole life. He raised a hand to wipe away a single tear. "Young man," he said. "I saw your picture in the papers."

"He's not a thief, Daddy," I hollered. "He was trying to stop Bud."

My father dropped his head. Then he extended his hand and looked Mick straight in the eye. "What I meant to say was, I saw you bravely try to stop Bud at the cabin the day he kidnapped you both. Thank you for bringing my daughter home safely. I owe you."

My sister kissed me on the side of the face and hugged me close. I felt a hand yank my hair and turned to see my brother. He was crying too. He didn't say he missed me or he loved me or anything, but he didn't have to. Next I felt Mama and I turned to her arms. Pressing against her softness, I felt safe at last. My days on the run were over.

These people. I'd never take them for granted again.

My father waved to the people waiting in the car. "Thank you so much. Thank you so much."

"Margaret, let's go closer," my mother said, "and you can introduce us."

As my father came up beside me, he whispered, "Is that that well-known spiritual singer?"

"Yes, Daddy," We approached the passenger side of the Packard.

"I've got more than a few exciting stories to tell you."

DR. JEROME LYLES

My head wobbled from sleep deprivation as I drove along the road home. Up ahead, I could see a red Packard with a white top slowing to turn into our front gate. I knew someone from the church was bringing Mick home. But who? No one at our church had the money to drive an automobile like that.

As they approached the house, my wife and two daughters came out on the porch followed by two men in suits. I adjusted my glasses to see better. It was Mick's father, Lucky, and his Uncle Robert. Why in the world had the two men not gone on to meet the private investigator?

The door to the Packard opened and Mick got out. Another person emerged from the other side of the auto. He put a cowboy hat on his head and hung back, as the crowd on the porch pushed forward toward Mick.

I pulled my truck up behind the Packard on the drive. My old friend Lucky had his arms around his son—no fighting, no arguing today. Robert stood near them, and Olivia and the girls looked on with beaming faces. Inside the auto, I saw Thomas and Sister Rosetta, the couple who were staying in the guest rooms at the church during their Dallas spiritual tour. I would have to find a way to repay them. Maybe Olivia would send them one of her cakes. I would see.

But first, I needed to check on Mick. Margaret had told me during her phone call yesterday that Bud had thrown him down so hard outside the gas station she could hear his head crack when it hit the hard ground.

"Mick," I said as I got out of my truck. "I need to check you for a concussion."

MICK

The sun slipped out of sight, and all around us lights blazed to life. Night in Deep Ellum is something to see, that's for sure. On the street, I made sure my mouth wasn't hanging open in awe. My heart pounded as we approached the club. I could feel the pulsing rhythm of the music inside my chest.

Cowboy wasn't wearing his hat tonight. And I had pomaded my wavy locks down in an attempt to disguise myself. We'd both taken a bath and washed our clothes. Since Cowboy only had one set of clothes, Dr. Lyles had loaned him some pants to wear while his dried. But they fit him so well, the doctor went ahead and gave them to him. Said they were getting tight in the stomach. I had to admit, Cowboy did look good. I saw several females giving him the eye as we made our way down the bustling sidewalk.

Still, my confidence faltered as we waited to enter the club door.

"Near capacity," the giant bouncer called out to us. Then he smiled and said, "However, I think we can fit two more." It was a warm night, and slightly muggy. His dark skin glistened in the glow from the street lamp. He held up his hand as he opened the door and made a sweeping gesture for us to enter.

When he opened the door and the full force of the music hit me, excitement lurched throughout my entire being. Cowboy sauntered in first. I straightened my shoulders and moistened my dry mouth. The bouncer made the sweeping entry gesture again. "You boys musicians?"

"Yessir," I answered with a frog in my throat. "Why do you ask?" I reached up and stroked the start of my new mustache hoping he didn't recognize me.

He grinned down from the heavens. "You look like musicians, that's why."

I grinned up at him, wondering how many fights he'd had as bouncer. I didn't dare ask.

"I bet you guys are good. You gonna play tonight?"

"No, we're going to buy a guitar from Sister Rosetta's friend Joe."

"Well, good luck to you." He looked at his pocket watch. "Better hurry and get yourself a seat. Sister Rosetta's up next."

I stepped inside the dimly lit room. Cowboy, who'd gone in first, was nowhere to be seen. I stood just inside, to the left of the door, and let my eyes adjust. Smoke hung like a fog in the single spotlight beam. A saxophone wailed. I couldn't have felt more at home.

Cowboy came up behind me. "I've got us a table over there."

We headed toward the empty table he'd gotten in the back of the bar, but before we could get there a couple in fancy clothes sat down. We decided to stand against the wall and watch the show from there.

After a round of heartfelt applause, the saxophone player left the stage. The lights dipped very low. When they came back up, our new friend stood on the stage holding her guitar. Behind her, the shadows of a backup group and a couple of big-band type musicians.

"Good evening, brothers and sisters," Rosetta said into the microphone. The crowd went wild with applause. She motioned for quiet. "Let me make sure my guitar is ready."

The crowd waited as she made a few tuning adjustments. When she had the sound just like she wanted it she said, "My name is Sister Rosetta . . . and I'm going to make a joyful noise tonight!" The crowd went wild again. With that, she ripped a few chords on her brand-spanking-new frying-pan electric guitar. The crowd yelled so loud, I swear the roof was shaking. I couldn't believe it. I'd heard of electrified stringed instruments but had never seen one in person.

When the roar from her fans decreased, she turned to the people on stage behind her, "Are you ready?" They nodded. Then she addressed the crowd. "Are you ready?"

The crowd screamed yes in unison.

Then she began to swing, beginning with a spiritual number she'd performed at church the time I saw her last. Only now, she was moving across the stage in a rocking rhythm movement, wailing on that electric guitar the whole time. The crowd rose to their feet, swaying and clapping in time. I thought of Bertha Sinclair's comment about Sister Rosetta reaching the sinners with her music. Some were certainly listening tonight.

I knew Cowboy had only come to buy his guitar, but I could tell he was impressed. At one point, he yelled something at me with a smile on his face, but I couldn't hear anything really except Sister Rosetta and her swinging band.

* * *

Joe put the guitar out on the table in Sister Rosetta's dressing room. It was a Martin D45. Not very many existed, and the few that did were expensive. Cowboy picked the instrument up and examined the pearl inlay.

"Why are you selling this beauty?" he asked.

"I need the money," Joe said. "My mama's done got sick and my wife has a baby coming. I have several good guitars I can use at gigs. But, if I can't sell this here guitar, I'm going to have to get a day job. And being a musician yourself . . . you realize how hard that is on a fella."

Cowboy put the guitar in position to play. "May I?"

"Of course." Joe sat down to listen.

As expected, Cowboy played to impress. Then he slowed it down and made it soft and mellow. The tune was haunting, and I watched the expressions on the few people around us as heartache came to the forefront of their minds. He was as good as any guitarist I'd ever heard—

and I'd made it my business to hear a lot.

"It's a beautiful guitar," Cowboy said. "But I'm afraid I don't have enough money for something like this. Do you want to sell one of your other guitars?"

"No, son. I need to sell this one for the price it can bring. It's got a hardshell case, be good for traveling to gigs."

"It'd be a good show guitar," I said. "You'd definitely be a star."

"I'm asking a hundred dollars for it."

Cowboy shook his head. Joe starting putting the guitar in its case.

"Wait." I pulled off my shoe and took out a hundred-dollar bill. Everyone in the room fell silent.

I pushed the money toward Cowboy. He shook his head. "I'll never be able to repay you."

I looked at the shocked faces in the room, then lowered my voice. "May we talk privately outside for a moment?" I left the hundred in Joe's hand as Cowboy followed me to the door. Sister Rosetta, who had watched the whole scenario unfold, gave me a curious look. "We'll only be a minute," I said.

She raised an eyebrow. "Take your time."

Once outside, Cowboy said under his breath, "I can't take no sin money."

"What do you mean?"

"I know where you got the money. Helping that outlaw in the filling-station holdup."

"I got it from my Dad," I replied, my face reddening. "He always carries a hundred on him, and my grandfather did the same. It's a family tradition. You can ask him tonight when we get back to the doctor's house."

Cowboy took hold of my arm. "You promise this ain't sin money, McLaren?"

"It's not. Please," I implored, "you helped Margaret and myself survive a bad situation. I want to repay you."

He opened the door, shaking his head. "McLaren, I can't take this guitar. I don't have access to the kind of money where I can ever pay you back."

"Then how 'bout I buy it for myself and let you use it for your shows."

It was obvious he was thinking hard. Finally he nodded yes.

"Okay," I said. "Let's go buy our guitar."

We went back inside Sister Rosetta's dressing room.

* * *

It was decided that Thomas would drive us back to the Lyles' house from the club. In the next few days, Cowboy and I would leave for Dalhart, where Sister Rosetta had arranged for us to stay with her friend and for Cowboy to play a few gigs. The thought of riding the boxcar again was rough, but we didn't want to call attention to ourselves—staying in the background, moving behind the scenes was the way to go. At least until the detective my father had hired could bring in evidence that proved I was innocent.

Out on the street, I inhaled deeply. I could smell the engine smoke of nearby trains. The hum of people filled the air with occasional bursts of laughter. As the door to the club closed behind us, the pounding music subsided. My eyes adjusted to the street lights after being inside the dimly lit bar.

Walking beside Thomas and Cowboy, I felt good about getting out of trouble and finding direction for my life. Yesterday, my father had seemed somewhat open to me making music for a living. He even mentioned something about having other singers in the family history, and said that must have been where I picked up my musical gene. I can only imagine it must be some ancestor from way back because I never heard him say anything about anyone else but me having musical abilities. Maybe in time I'd find an opportunity to ask him more about it.

Cowboy moved the hardshell guitar case he was carrying from one hand to the other. By the way he was smiling, I knew he felt like a kid on Christmas morning. I sure hoped he'd let me play the thing once in a while. I wasn't in his league, but I wasn't half bad either.

Up ahead, outside a domino parlor, a nattily dressed black man on a wooden crate strummed a Gibson. His vocals and playing were so sorrowful, they made my heart twist up in my chest something awful. We all stopped to listen. The guitarist was singing about prison. Maybe that's why it affected me so powerfully—the words hit a little too close to home. Going to prison scared me so bad, I thought I might take my own life rather than face the hardships inside. I remembered Elvin talking to Bud when we were sitting outside on the porch in Fate, about how prison had hardened him. Bud had agreed, but said he didn't know how to go back to being his old self. He'd told Elvin he was too far gone.

I hung my head and let the man's blues wash over me. Thomas and Cowboy were held spellbound, too.

When he finished his song, Thomas tossed some coins in the guitar case that sat on the ground beside him. I saw the last name "Johnson" printed in white letters on the side.

"Hey, Robert," Thomas said. "Where's old Lead Belly been hiding himself?"

"Man, Huddie got himself in some trouble down in Louisiana. He's biding his time in the Big House even as we speak."

"For what?"

"I don't rightly know," Robert continued to strum while talking to us. "All I know is somebody told me Lead Belly's doing time down in

Louisiana at the Angola Prison Farm." The man cocked his head to the side as he spoke, listening to the music coming from his fingers.

"He's doing hard time?" Thomas asked.

"Yep," Robert continued. "Also heard he's been making recordings while he's in there. At least he's not wasting away. Heard tell he may be getting out any day now for good behavior."

"I sure miss him. And I miss Blind Lemon." Thomas stared off down the street at a group of people coming out of a restaurant. Their voices floated in the night air.

"I miss 'em, too. Can't believe Blind Lemon's been dead near five years now." Robert lowered his eyes as he spoke.

"I know you miss 'em. We all do." Thomas put his hand on the other man's shoulders, giving him what comfort he could. "But you know what?" His soft voice lightened the heavy conversation. "You blues singers need to learn how to stay out of prison." Thomas gave Robert a playful slap on the back and Robert laughed.

Changing the subject, Thomas took the opportunity to introduce us. "Boys, this here's the best Delta blues player Mississippi ever churned out. He's truly something different. Heard tell he went down to the crossroads and sold his soul to the devil so he could play like that. Is that true, Robert?"

Robert turned a million-dollar smile in our direction as he ripped sounds from the strings like I'd never heard. He never answered, just continued playing in the background of our conversation. Never missed a beat. It was clear he was happy to see Thomas.

Turning his attention back to us, Thomas continued, "Robert, this is Cowboy." Then he pointed in my direction, "And this is Sundown." I startled at the sound of my new alias. Where in the world had Thomas come up with Sundown? I liked it.

"Nice to meet you boys." Robert shook our hands before returning to his guitar. "I'd like to hear you play sometime."

"They're going to be in West Texas for a while," Thomas said. "But they'll be back shortly and look you up."

"You do that," he said as we waved our goodbyes. "I'll show you a thing or two about the Blues." I had no doubt he would, and I was more than willing to learn.

When we were out of earshot of Robert, Thomas told us Robert was going to be big someday. "Did you notice that 'chucka chucka' rhythm he was making? Ain't never met nobody that can make sounds come out of a guitar like he does. Did you see how smoothly he moved from hen-picking to bottleneck slides? He's always making up new stuff." Thomas stopped and wiped his brow with a handkerchief as we came up to his automobile, "I swear, sometimes the guy makes his guitar sound like he's playing two guitars at once."

"Do you really think he made a deal with the Devil?" Cowboy grinned at Thomas and me when he said it.

"Don't know." Thomas smiled back and unlocked his automobile for us to get inside. "Someone that knows Robert well told me he couldn't play for nothing, then all of a sudden he upped and became a musical genius." He shrugged his shoulders as he started the car. "So, who knows. But it makes a good story, don't it?"

Thomas was right about one thing. The guitarist on the corner was really something. As we drove back up the street with our car windows rolled down, I noticed a crowd had gathered round this man, and even though I couldn't see him, I could still hear the rawness of his voice wailing out into the night. The sound would stay with me a long time.

5 HOT TIMES IN THE PANHANDLE

MICK

Thomas took us back to the Lyles' house so I could get my guitar and my small bag of clothes. Uncle Robert had purchased two train tickets for us to Dalhart, so we wouldn't have to hop a boxcar after all. Of course, my father gave me spending money. He also took me aside and told me he thought it best if I laid low in the sparsely populated region where I was headed. Uncle Robert stepped in and translated for me in no uncertain terms. "Don't go anywhere, don't do anything, and don't talk to anyone—not even the rattlesnakes and horned toads."

I appreciated all my father and Uncle Robert had been doing, as far as trying to prove my innocence. The private investigator was working overtime on the case, but so far nothing was coming up in my favor. In fact, a few people had come forward to testify they had witnessed me in an earlier holdup. Which of course was not true. I'd never stolen anything in my life—I didn't even know what was going on in that filling station when I walked in to buy gum. It was only once the attendant had the cash drawer open that Bud came up behind me and pulled his gun. When he shot the man and took the money, I pulled my gun and chased Bud out of the store. I hated to think of it. It made my heart hurt.

Why hadn't I listened to Olivia when she asked me to leave Dr. Lyles' gun at home?

I watched Cowboy getting his things together. He was so excited about getting to ride first class, he was almost giddy. To tell the truth, it made me feel guilty that I'd gone first class for as long as I could remember. I glanced over at my father and his worried eyes met mine. "Now, you stay hidden son," he said. "Remember when you kids were little and your momma used to show you how to hide in a place where there was no place to hide?"

I nodded.

"Well, you bring out that knowledge and use it wisely. I know when she showed you it was all in fun, but it could save your life. Not every kid had a mother who was a spy in the Great War." He laughed as he said it. But it was true. My Italian mother had been an Allied spy before she came to America.

Thinking of my mother made me sadder. I needed to be positive for the people who were going to great lengths to help me. For one thing, I was thankful Cowboy had decided to keep me company. I know he was mainly going because he wanted the money from the gig. But he believed in my innocence, and that carried weight with me.

Cowboy, of course, could go anywhere he pleased in Dalhart. He couldn't wait to meet Sister Rosetta's musician friends so he could start getting paid professionally. He had told me earlier that, seeing as Dalhart was near the border of Oklahoma, it would be easy for him to visit home and give his Dad and brothers some cash. He said last time he saw them the crops had all but dried up on their drought-ridden farm near Guymon.

* * *

It had been decided that Thomas would pick us up and take us to the train, since not many people knew him—as opposed to Dr. Lyles, who knew almost everyone in town. I certainly didn't want to damage the doctor's reputation by having people see him with me. My father and Uncle Robert didn't even attempt to come, as everyone in Texas knew it was Lucky McLaren's son in the hold-up photo from the newspaper.

So here we were riding toward the trainyard—me disguised in a hat and reading glasses—and we could see a group of people outside waiting on the station platform. As we drew closer, I could also see policemen checking the passengers. Thomas told me to get down in the backseat floorboard as he cruised by the chaotic scene.

"Do you think they're looking for us?" Cowboy said under his breath.

"Maybe," Thomas answered. "Someone might've recognized Mick's uncle when he bought the tickets. They could've guessed he was buying a ticket for his nephew."

Cowboy opened the door. "I'll go ask someone in the crowd what's happening."

"No," Thomas said. "Let me. Don't forget your name is on one of those tickets."

From the backseat floorboard, I kneeled and peeked out the window. "Look over there." I pointed to the west. "That freight train two tracks over is headed in the right direction. I could hop a boxcar and meet you in the Panhandle, Cowboy."

"No," he said. "I'm used to riding boxcars and you ain't. Get your guitar and let's go."

"You don't have to ask me twice." I jumped out beside him.

"I wish you luck," Thomas hollered after us. As we ran toward the rolling freight train, I looked back to wave. But Thomas was already turning his car around to head in the other direction.

Cowboy selected an almost-empty car for us. As he attempted to board with his new guitar, I noticed he was particularly careful about going up the boxcar ladder. It didn't take him long to get on board safely and hide his guitar behind some interior bales of hay.

Now it was my turn. I lifted my guitar inside from my position on the exterior ladder, and it bounced dangerously close to the side of the rolling boxcar before coming to a rest. Without a second's hesitation, I gave it a hard shove back inside and hoisted myself up. Magically, Cowboy appeared from around the hay bales and grabbed me and my guitar, pulling me to safety.

Cowboy propped his back up against a hay bale and stretched out his long legs on the dirty floor. "Make yourself comfortable, Sundown." He pulled his straw hat down over his eyes. "It's going to be a long ride."

"Dagnabbit," I said. "I hate that we had to hop a freight train. I know how much you wanted to ride first class in the passenger train my Uncle Robert had booked us tickets for."

"Naw. If I rode first class once, I'd always know what I was missing."

MARGARET

My sister Samantha was listening to the radio, as she did most days while we worked in the house. However, today was a special day for our family. Momma had told her to get the dining-room table ready for Easter lunch. We absolutely never used the expensive table or china in the dining room, but today it seems we were going to. I wondered if we were having company, but Samantha said, "Momma had decided we needed to use and appreciate the few nice things we have."

My sister picked up a feather duster, pretending it was a microphone. Twirling about to the latest hit song, she mouthed the words to "I Only Have Eyes For You." I knew it was one of her favorite songs, so I stopped to watch her. Samantha was always fun to watch.

She looked so pretty today, dressed in her Sunday best with her hair all braided up nice. She had seen the hair style in a magazine and pasted it on her vanity mirror just last week. Momma surprised her yesterday with two ribbons to weave through her braids, so she could copy the look exactly.

Speaking of surprises for Samantha, I had one planned too. It was April first, I had concocted the perfect April Fool's prank with her in mind. But now I was having second thoughts. For some reason, the time didn't seem right. Maybe I'd try later. But then that'd give Samantha time to get an April Fool's prank over on me first—and I couldn't have that.

I had just decided to attempt to pull off my joke when she turned to me. "Mama needs help in the kitchen."

I stayed seated right where I was and watched as she continued to dance with her imaginary partner. "Are you deaf, girl? You need to go help Momma."

"I know," I said. "But life is too short not to take a moment to oneself every now and then."

She turned the radio's volume up a notch. Then she brought her feather duster microphone over to me and said, "You take it from here."

Just as the last verse began, I stood up and sang along from memory. "Oh, Margaret," Samantha said as the song ended, a hint of pride in her voice. "You do have the most beautiful voice. You should enter the talent show down at . . ."

Just then, a newsman broke in.

"We have an important public address report out of Grapevine, Texas. Wanted fugitives Clyde Barrow and Bonnie Parker, along with Henry Methvin, are believed to be responsible for the deaths of two young highway patrolmen this morning. Initial reports from eye witnesses indicate that before the officers could draw their guns, they were shot dead in cold blood. Law enforcement officials have vowed to bring these wanted criminals in, dead or alive. If you should encounter these dangerous individuals or anyone associated with them, contact your local police force immediately."

I sat down. It took a full minute for the words to make sense. I remembered Doreen's face. "Tell the world something good about me."

Samantha tenderly put an arm around my shoulders. "It could've been you that was murdered. We could've lost you." I could hear the pain in her voice. She hugged me close, my head resting on her chest, just like Momma used to hold us when we were little girls.

I couldn't breathe. Not because of how tight Samantha was holding me, or out of fear for what could have happened, but because of the realization that Mick was now in even more danger. This last exploit would probably make people think they should take him dead or alive, too!

Finally I managed to get out the words. "What about Mick?"

Samantha just had a pained look in her eyes.

I pulled back from Samantha's embrace. "I've never felt about anyone the way I feel about Mick," I said. "My heart hurt the day we had to go our separate ways. Not that I wasn't plenty glad to see you all." I clasped hands to my chest and searched Samantha's face. "Right now my heart hurts through and through. It literally aches." I stopped for a moment, then continued. "Every waking moment, I think of him. Everything brings my thoughts back to him. What if I never see him again? How will I go on like this?"

Samantha stood and looked down at me. "Dear Lawd!" she said. "Margaret, you're in love. How did this happen? I was supposed to fall in love first. Have you kissed him yet?"

"Not on the lips," I replied. "But he did kiss me on the head. And he held my hand."

"Good," she said. "At least I have you beat there."

I looked up at her. "Who have you kissed on the lips?"

"Never you mind." She went back to dusting.

"Samantha, my whole world is falling apart and you're dusting."

"No, I'm thinking. Maybe we should go find the photographer who took the picture of Mick and sold it to the papers. If he also took photos of those two fighting, we could prove he's innocent."

"Mick's father has already sent a private investigator to find the photographer."

She stopped dusting and looked at the ceiling. I could tell her mind was working overtime.

"The investigator doesn't seem to be getting the job done." She set the duster down in a nearby chair. "Maybe we go to the photographer ourselves and tell him the whole story. Ask for his help. He'll remember seeing you there, I just know he'll talk with you. And he'll believe you, too!"

"But we can't drive," I said in dismay.

"No, but you know how to hop a freight car."

I looked at her like she was crazy. "Or we could take a bus like normal people. I've still got a little of the money Doreen gave me when Bud turned us loose in the cotton field."

"You know her real name is—"

I cut Samantha off. "She'll always be Doreen to me, and she isn't a cigar-toting moll. She doesn't even smoke cigars, just the occasional Camel cigarette when she could get them. And, something else." My sister stared, waiting for me to continue. "She had some really nice traits."

"Like what?"

"She was empathetic. She didn't let Bud kill us when he could've easily." I caught my breath. "You don't know Doreen. She was good-hearted in many ways."

"She sounds like a real peach." I thought Samantha was being sarcastic, but you never could tell. Sometimes my sister was a total mystery to me.

"Should we tell Momma we're going to find the photographer?" I asked.

"Or should we just go and come back the same day?" Samantha asked in return. "We'll pick a school day to go, so she won't miss us. We'll tell her we have to stay after school, to practice for the talent show."

MICK

Johnny Whiskey was a wiry little man with graying hair and beard. Sister Rosetta told us he was a good friend, and we'd been told he was a good piano player. But from observation, we knew he wasn't much of a talker.

However, he was a gracious host. After answering his door, he waved us back to his kitchen, where he was eating supper. Getting out two plates, he served up green beans and mashed potatoes, then put on carrots and some squash. "Sorry, boys," he said. "I don't have any meat to serve you. But I do have some fresh baked bread I bought from the family down the road.

"We didn't expect you to feed us," Cowboy said. "We'll pay you back."

"No," he said, "I made too much anyway. Used to cooking for a large family after my wife died. All the kids grown up and gone away."

I looked around the simple kitchen with its bare walls. Two long shelves held dishes, pots, and pans. Not many, but then how many dishes does one man need? The frame house itself was rather large and had been easy to spot from miles away, standing proud against the barren fields. I wondered if we'd be staying in the house or the barn. After all, he was letting us stay for free until Cowboy started playing gigs for money. I knew Sister Rosetta had explained my plight, and I hoped I could clear my name soon and start playing music in public.

We ate in silence. As he was clearing the dishes, Johnny asked, "Do you like that new Western Swing?"

I knew what he was talking about, and apparently Cowboy did too because he said, "I like what Bob Wills is doing. However, I've never played it."

"Would you be willing to try?"

We both said yes, though he was probably talking more to Cowboy than myself.

"Trying to get a group together. Practicing over back of the grain store tomorrow night. You're both welcome to come."

I hopped up from my chair and went to stand beside him at the sink. "Let me do the dishes. I won't feel right if we don't help."

"I guess we can do them together, like I used to when the kids were home. Don't have a lot of extra water, but I guess we've got enough to get the job done," he said as he dipped a big bowl in a water barrel and sat it down inside the sink.

"I'll scrape. Cowboy, you wash. And Mick you stand at the end of the line and dry."

With that he whipped out a flour-sack cup towel and put it in my hand.

We worked for a few minutes, making great time, when Cowboy said, "Boy, does this remind me of my time at home."

I kept silent. I don't think I'd ever dried a dish in my life. But I have to say, I was pretty good at it. I held up the spoon I was polishing and made sure there wasn't a speck on it.

"You from around here?" Johnny said to Cowboy.

"Yessir, from Guymon."

"You ought to go pay your folks a visit while you're so close."

Cowboy choked up a little. "Just my father now, and maybe one brother at home. But I would like to go see them. Visit my mother's grave."

* * *

Johnny Whiskey suggested he take us to Guymon in his truck, then we'd hop the train back to Dalhart. We'd taken him up on his offer, and it had been a smooth ride over the dirt roads. There were few potholes to contend with. We'd left our belongings at Johnny's house, as we were only going to stay a few hours. Cowboy wanted to be back in time to practice with the new band Johnny was trying to put together.

I had on a cowboy hat one of Johnny's many sons had left behind. "It fits you good," Cowboy said when he saw me in it. "Now pull it low so it shades your face." He adjusted the hat on my head. Johnny had given us both bandanas to tie in front of our mouths to keep the dust out as we drove, so I figured no one would guess who I was.

Cowboy's family farm was just this side of Guymon, so we weren't much more than an hour out. I could see railroad tracks along the way and figured it would be easy to get back to Dalhart. Then we'd just walk to Johnny's place. I was more than impressed he'd driven us without really knowing us.

Cowboy had filled up his tank with gas, but Johnny refused to let him pay for it. Said he needed to go into Guymon to see a man about a tractor. I didn't want to say anything, but there wasn't a lot growing out in this area of the country. Johnny could probably have his pick of tractors for little of nothing.

As if he could read my mind, Cowboy said, "Gosh darn, this drought has been going on for nearly four years. Never thought I'd say I'd wish it would rain."

"Going to take more than one rain to make things right around here," Johnny replied.

I thought back to when my Uncle Robert had brought me up through this part of the country, when we'd visited our grandparents near Amarillo. It must've been about seven years ago, but it'd been filled with prairie grasses and freshly plowed fields of wheat. Ironically enough, it had rained that day. I remember, Uncle Robert had to go extra slow over the slippery dirt roads. He'd complained about the rain the whole way up to Oklahoma.

* * *

"Come inside, Andy." It took me a moment to realize Cowboy's father was talking to him. Of course, I knew Cowboy Larson wasn't his real name. But I'd never thought to ask him about it. The older Larson looked just like his son except, of course, he had thinning hair and a few more wrinkles on his face and hands.

"Pa, this is my friend Mick. And that's Johnny Whiskey that dropped us off." Cowboy waved to Johnny as he turned his truck around in the road and headed the other way. "He's the man I told you about, that's helping me get work in the music business."

I pulled my bandana off my face and came forward to shake hands. His father seemed to think it was perfectly normal for us to have bandanas covering our mouths and noses. "You boys come inside" he said, "and tell me what you've been up to."

A table in the hallway was cluttered with newspapers and magazines. A headline stuck out at me, and I stopped. It read in bold letters: "Bonnie Parker and Clyde Barrow Kill Two Patrolmen Near Grapevine, Texas" Cowboy saw it too and picked up the paper to read the entire story.

His father gave him a moment before saying, "That's a sad story, ain't it? Happened a few days ago on Easter Sunday. Heard one of the officers was about to get married, first day on the job when they killed him. The fiancée wore her wedding dress to the funeral."

My blood ran cold, and I had trouble concentrating the rest of the visit. But Cowboy—I mean *Andy*—didn't seem to notice, so happy was he to catch up with his dad. I watched in a blur as they brought out photographs and went over family memories. Then we all walked down to the nearby cemetery and picked what few wildflowers we could find to leave on his mother's grave. The mound of dirt on her plot had not had time to sink even with the other ground yet. Though no one had inscribed her actual death date on the granite tombstone, I knew it couldn't have happened long ago.

"Enid wouldn't like weeds." The older Larson bent and pulled a few from the foot of her grave. "She liked to keep everything tidy."

Andy stooped by his father and straightened the concrete blocks outlining the grave. As he stood up he said, "One thing I remember about mother was that she was always combing my hair into place. That, and making sure my pants were pulled up just so or my collar was straight. It used to drive me crazy."

He arranged the wildflowers he'd picked at the front of her tombstone. "Now I'm constantly combing my own hair into place," he said. I stepped back to let him talk privately. "It's all your fault, Mother. Look what you did to us kids. You made us unable to stand dirt. And now we have this horrible, horrible dust to contend with. We can't escape it. Silt everywhere, no reprieve. I'm glad you're in Heaven and don't have to deal with it."

Mr. Larson moved closer and put his hand on his son's shoulder. "Enid, I love you. But it's getting time for these boys to hop the train back to Dalhart."

He turned to me. "Watch out for the Railroad Police, I hear they've been eyeing Dalhart something fierce, to keep people moving on to California instead of stopping in Texas. Can't say as I blame them. Texas isn't much better off than Oklahoma."

* * *

Later, on the boxcar to Dalhart, we sat cross-legged with our backs against the metal wall. We could feel every jolt of the train as it rambled down the steel tracks. The hum of the engine echoed through every cell in our bodies. Without a doubt this was going to be one of our more uncomfortable rides. But we couldn't complain because we weren't paying customers and it sure beat walking.

I could tell something was weighing heavy on Cowboy's heart. I thought it was his mother's recent death, but I was wrong. Finally, he looked up and pushed his hat back on his head.

"Mick, did Margaret tell you about what the saleswoman said when we were buying shoes in Dallas?"

"No," I said. "But I did notice Margaret had replaced her mother's torn-up shoes with new ones."

Cowboy stretched his legs out. "We went to this shoe store to get Margaret some shoes. I'd been to this particular store before, with my father and brothers when we came down to Dallas on a trip once. The same saleslady that waited on our family then was still working there. Of course, she doesn't recognize me after all this time. But at the time of my family's visit she was making a big deal out of the fact we'd come all the way from Oklahoma to visit her shoe store. Told us how her sister had just moved to Tulsa. On and on she went about how proud she was to sell us boots." He stopped and took the ever-present matchstick from between his lips. "So, the other day when she's waiting on Margaret and me, the same saleslady starts talking about all those Okies coming down, over-running the place. Making fun of how poor the Okies were these days and how some of them were even tying newspapers around their feet because they couldn't afford shoes. She actually said, 'I don't want no Okies in our store.' I couldn't believe it, because she was still waiting on the two of us and it was obvious she didn't know where I was from."

He stopped talking and pulled his hat down over his eyes. "Her words hurt me deep. She stripped me of whatever pride I had left, and she doesn't even know it. That saleslady doesn't know the half of what people like me and my folks have been through. We may have fallen on hard times, but we're still the same people we were a few years back. Just poorer, that's all."

"Don't let some old gossiping bitty hurt you."

Even as I said it, I knew it rang hollow. The woman's words had wounded Cowboy in a way he wasn't going to recover from anytime soon.

Before too long, he took his hat off and ran his fingers through his hair, much as I'm sure his mother used to do when he was younger.

"I sure wish I had my guitar with me," he said.

MARGARET

Being the model child in our family, Samantha could never do anything wrong. So I knew our parents wouldn't be suspicious when she said she was taking me to a talent competition. Mother got so excited about the prospect of me being in a talent show, I felt guilty. Maybe I really would try out. There was still time.

As we boarded the bus to Cooper, Texas, to go find the photographer, I turned to Samantha. "I hope no one tells Mother the talent show tryouts are really next week."

"Why would they? No one suspects she has a talented child."

I laughed. "I wish I really did have the guts to try out for the talent show. One side of me really wants to sing in front of people, and the other side is afraid someone will laugh at me."

"Some might laugh because they're jealous, but you've got a beautiful singing voice. If you're going to be a star, you need to get past your fears."

I thought about what Sister Rosetta had said about no one believing in you if you can't believe in yourself. I thought about Mick and Cowboy, hitching boxcars to Dallas to pursue their dreams. Both took wild risks. Then I thought of myself, afraid to get up on stage at a local talent show. My ambitions seemed trivial. But one person believed in me, and that was Samantha.

Looking around from our seats near the back of the bus, I observed the passengers in front of us. It was hard to believe the bus was already rolling down the highway; it seemed like we had just purchased our tickets. Clutching my purse, I made certain the rest of the money Doreen had given me was still there. "Hey," I said, "Did you know one of the highway patrolman that got killed on Easter Sunday was engaged to be married?"

Samantha gasped in horror.

"His fiancée attended his funeral in her wedding dress." As I said the words, I thought of Doreen asking me to say something good about her. But I couldn't after I read that. I just couldn't.

Then I remembered Mick and Bud's photo, and I knew all was not always what it seemed. A person had to get the facts. No, I told myself, don't judge Doreen yet.

ANTONIA

Being a mother is never easy. But waiting to hear word on our missing child was the worst kind of pain I'd ever endured. Every telephone call, every knock at the door caused a nervous jolt of panic. When I woke in the morning, my thoughts were immediately heavy. It was the not knowing. Not being able to do anything.

Lucky and Robert had tried to find the photographer, but it was a dead end. Margaret must have been wrong about hearing the camera continuing as the action played out. Lucky said the people in town wouldn't give up the photographer's identity. One teacher at the nearby school said to Lucky, "It looked to me like your son robbed the station."

But I knew Mick wouldn't have been a part of the robbery willingly. He probably had more money in his shoe than the man had in his cash register. Besides, Mick was extraordinarily kind—very empathetic.

Sitting in the living room, I looked up at our family portrait. Sure, he had a mischievous streak, but he was never cruel. Just full of energy and life. Even as a child he was loving and spontaneous. I never knew if he was going to strip naked and jump in a pond or roll a bag of oranges one at a time down the grand staircase. He was always up to something. Everyone loved his boyish charm.

Perhaps Lucky loved him most of all. He took Mick and André

with him into the oilfields, teaching them every aspect of the business. Clearly he intended for them to join him and Robert when they got older. All he ever wanted was to give them a good life, but he was pushing way too hard. He told me he'd taken the doctor's advice not to scold or chastise Mick when he and Robert had visited Mick and Cowboy in Dallas. He said he was trying to let Mick go his own way.

Then I thought of Lucky and his own ambitions. He'd wanted to run for governor since he returned from the war almost sixteen years ago. This was supposed to be his time to shine, to fulfill his dreams. But the photograph of Mick and Bud had squashed those dreams in less than twenty-four hours. The whole state was up in arms over it. He couldn't expect anyone to vote for him when no one was talking to us.

I suspected that he was not going to announce his bid to run as he'd planned.

MICK

The night air had grown downright chilly as we flew through the night on steel rails. Cowboy had helped me push the big metal door closed earlier. Now the boxcar was dark, and we sat in silence.

My musings turned to Margaret. I don't know what I'd thought about before I met her. Now every little thing made me think of her, want to talk to her, want to be near her. "I've got a girl back in Oklahoma," Cowboy said suddenly, as if he knew who I was dreaming about.

"What's her name?"

"Her name is Saint. It's a nickname, of course, but it's what everyone calls her. She's real pretty. Real name is Dove LaReaux. She's part French and part Cherokee."

"Where is she now?"

"Her mother died and her father couldn't take care of her and her siblings. Put her in the Indian Boarding School at Newkirk, near the Kansas border. I suppose it's the best thing for her. She gets fed regular meals, has clean sheets to lay her head on at night. She's getting a good education. He stopped talking and I could hear him moving around to a more comfortable position. After a while he added, "I sure miss her." Then he stopped talking again.

So many people my age had already lost their parents. A twinge of guilt stabbed at me. My mother was probably worried sick. She was the kind that waited up every night until both André and myself came home. Maybe I should send her a postcard without a return address, just something to let her know I was alive and staying out of trouble.

* * *

When we pulled into Dalhart, I stretched and prepared to jump from the train. Before we could slide open the metal door, it opened for us—the rusty metal clanging as it moved, achingly slowly.

Cowboy stood back in the shadows. I crept up to the inside corner, near the door. Using my feet to climb some steel bolts on the wall, I moved myself up over the door opening, where I clung to two rods from the ceiling. Whoever was out there would have to be looking hard to see me up here in the ceiling of the freight car.

The barrels of two rifles greeted Cowboy.

Slowly one of the gun owners moved around to where I could see his face.

The other moved into view.

I believed the men to be the railroad police Cowboy's father had cautioned us about. One of them had a star on his pocket. Maybe they were local law.

The tallest officer had a dark mustache and a white Stetson pulled down over his eyes. He was the first to speak. "Dalhart can't take on anymore vagrants—best be moving on to California. We ain't got room here. So don't even think about getting off this train."

I couldn't tell if he had spotted me, or if he was only addressing Cowboy. The second man put down his gun and offered Cowboy a single sack lunch.

"Here's some food to tide you over." He pushed the sack onto the boxcar floor before retreating. By the look in his eyes, he was uncomfortable with his job.

The second man gestured toward Cowboy with his gun.

"Don't get off the train. Just keep going till you reach the land of milk and honey. Lots of work for you out in California, I'm told."

I wanted to tell him I was a Texan from down near Houston way. But I knew by this time they still hadn't seen me. And, even if they had that'd be leaving Cowboy in the lurch, and I didn't want to do that as he was just about my only friend in the world right now.

The man with the white hat slammed the big steel door shut, leaving us in the dark again.

Neither of us moved as we listened to the two men retreat. When the train start to roll again, we knew what we needed to do. As quiet as we could, we slid the door open just enough to leap out. Cowboy went first and made a perfect landing. I went second and fell on my side, dropping the sack lunch. The landing hurt my right hand, hopefully not so bad I couldn't play guitar.

After I'd regained my footing, we headed toward a building that appeared to be a dry goods store or a warehouse. Above us, the moon was a sliver. The night cloaked everything like velvet. Once in a while, I caught a flash of Cowboy's silver belt buckle as he turned back to look at me. I wished he'd stop for a moment and let us get our bearings.

We hadn't been off the train for three minutes when we heard someone rack their gun.

The officer didn't have to tell us to put our hands in the air. We did it automatic. But the owner of the gun decided he needed to speak any ways. "Boys," he said in a deep voice. "Did I not just tell you to stay on the train?" Keeping his gun trained at our chests, he came up on the side of us. "Now I have to take you to jail."

The clouds slipped from in front of the moon, and I could see the man in the white hat a little better. He pointed his rifle at the building in front of us. "The jail is just around the corner."

My feet hurt. My hand hurt. Most of all, my pride hurt. We stumbled around the corner of the building. Behind me I heard the second officer as he caught up with the first.

"There's two of 'em. Where in the sam hill did this second one come from?"

6 ON THE ROAD TO NOWHERE

ANTONIA

My nine-year-old daughter Katherine needed me. She was getting stronger every day, but she still had a long way to go.

The pain of seeing her in the Iron Lung for those two weeks last year will always haunt me. Even as a former nurse, I wasn't prepared to see my baby in the cumbersome contraption. But it saved her life, and for that I'm eternally grateful.

Truly, it is a miracle of modern-day medicine. I can still remember how wispy her voice sounded. She could only talk on the exhale of the machine, and that forced her to choose her words carefully. Our conversations were interrupted about fifteen times per minute. She later said it taught her patience.

My beautiful, beautiful girl. So much like her father, always finding the best in every situation. They even laughed about the braces on her leg and his artificial leg from his war injury. She inherited her steel resolve from him.

Only once in our marriage did I ever hear Lucky complain about his war injuries. It was when his head ached and he was suffering from double-vision in his one good eye. There was little the doctor could do for him except knock him out with pain medication. Apparently it didn't work well. For two days, he stayed in a darkened room with cool rags over his eyes.

I knew he hid the pain he felt most days, and I hoped tiny Katherine wouldn't have to do the same. Glancing over at her, I noticed how similar she looked to her father. The same bright blue eyes and dark wavy hair that had attracted me to him years ago. She even held her mouth in the same determined position as she worked through her therapy exercises. I tried to concentrate on her progress, yet thoughts of Mick kept breaking through to torture me. What if he never returned home? Would I be able to live with this dull ache inside?

The door to Katherine's room opened and Bobby, my youngest son, came in. His cheeks were pink from playing outside in the heat. His sandy-colored hair was damp and cherubic curls clung to his face. Unlike Katherine, he was tall and strong for his age.

"I'm hungry," he said. "Will you come down and make me a sandwich?"

"Juliet is quite capable of making you a sandwich. After all, she studied at one of the best cooking schools in France. That's why your father hired her to cook for us."

"I know." He came over to me and sat in my lap. "But you make it better."

MICK

The Dalhart Hilton was full when we checked into our jail cells that evening. Everywhere I looked, my eyes alighted on a homeless vagrant or a down-on-his-luck migrant worker. I guess Cowboy and I weren't the only two that tried their luck at getting off the train here in town. The man with the star on his chest opened the less full of the two holding rooms with bars, and more or less shoved us inside.

Our cell had a sink and a toilet. The walls were lined with hard wooden benches. Three men sat up on one bench. A fourth was sleeping on the wooden floor, using his bindle bag as a pillow. A fifth younger one sat alone with his head buried in his hands. His discouraged posture bore down on me. At his feet sat a small sack full of life's necessities.

It surprised me that all the inmates around us still had what little belongings they'd brought in with them. In the cell across the way, one man had a wheelbarrow full of stuff. In fact, I still had the sack lunch in my hand that the kinder of the two railroad detectives had given me when they told us to keep riding.

The young dejected-looking guy swung his head up. "Sir, I'll trade you a nickel for that sack lunch." He didn't even know what was in it, yet I could tell he wanted it in a bad way. I figured he must have been given the same kind of sack lunch when he was captured hoboing. Which lead me to wonder if they would feed us in here.

"You can have it." I extended the bag in his direction.

He rummaged through it and brought out a sandwich then reached into his pocket and brought out a shiny nickel.

"No, you take it."

"Sure you don't want a nickel?" he said as he devoured the sandwich. "You could go to the cinema, watch that new Marx Brothers. Escape your suffering for a little while."

I sat down beside the boy I'd given the food. He looked to be about two years younger than me. "My name's Sundown," I said aloud to all the people in our cell. "And this is my friend Cowboy."

"I'm Otto," said the young boy.

The men on the bench scooted to make room for Cowboy.

"I'm Jim, this is Keith and this is Simon," said the older of the three men. "George is sleeping on the floor."

No one spoke for a full two minutes. Otto chewed softly, not missing a single crumb.

When he finished, he turned and said, "I'm not a railroad bum or a drifter. I've been crisscrossing the country, following the harvest. Shakin' walnuts, pickin' beans and strawberries, hoeing hops. Whatever I can do to make a little money. I was trying to catch a ride out to California, got turned around and headed down into Texas. And these two here"—he pointed through the bars at the men who'd brought us in—"picked me up for vagrancy."

The two men glanced casually over in our direction but continued their conversation.

"We're musicians," I said. "Trying to get back to our gig. I'm actually from Houston." This last part I said loud enough for the officers to hear. Slowly, but surely the man with the star made his way over to the front of our cell. "That's a good line of talk, Sundown. Why don't you tell me your real name?"

* * *

Roaming. Wandering. Hurting. These tough times made a harsh existence for people everywhere, but I have to say, being rescued from jail by your grandmother is not something I would wish on anyone.

It shouldn't have surprised me my grandmother Sarah Michelle, or Nana Michelle as we grandkids liked to call her, would come to save me. After all, she was one of the most capable women in the world. She wasn't physically strong, but she had nerves of steel and an unwavering faith the Lord would pull her through even the toughest of circumstances. No matter what adversity came her way, her attitude was always one of enduring hope.

Once, when I asked her where her courage came from she said, "I'm not courageous, I just go ahead and do what I need to do even though I'm afraid. The fear melts away eventually." Then she added, "I have faith in a higher being."

I remember her standing at the kitchen counter, stirring batter. "Mick," she said. "You don't have to believe in a higher power, but I can assure you that you'll have a tough go of it on your own." This kind of positive spiritual thinking alongside the fact she was always Johnny-on-the-spot in an emergency made her the kind of person you wanted to have on your side. Truth be told, I almost called her last night instead of Dr. Lyles, but I didn't want to wake her up and cause her undue worry. But Dr. Lyles or my father must have thought to call her because here she was in person, come to save the day—or at least my hide.

It'd only taken a few seconds for the name Mick McLaren to register with the lawman.

Of course, it made sense for her to come and get me as she lived on a ranch outside of Amarillo. But still, she was my grandmother. I didn't want her to think ill of me, didn't want her to view me as the one who was always getting in trouble. Even though I *was* always getting in trouble.

Thank goodness Nana Michelle wasn't the judging type.

From behind bars, I watched Nana Michelle. She wasted very little effort in her movements. Before the paperwork had even been started, she'd walked through the front door of the jail holding her head high. Going straight to the deputy sheriff's desk, she told him she'd come for her grandson. It was apparent the deputy knew who she was, too. After a few minutes of polite conversation, he said something to Nana Michelle so low I couldn't hear it. But I saw her hand him a small bag of what I could only assume was money.

As the deputy sheriff unlocked our cell, she came up behind him. "Come along boys." She waved us through the unlocked cell door as if we were toddlers on our way to the park.

"You only paid for one boy." The deputy sheriff held up a hand to halt Cowboy from exiting behind me.

Nana Michelle gave the deputy sheriff a steely look unlike I'd ever seen from her. "I'm taking both boys," she said between clenched teeth. "You can try and stop me. But I wouldn't advise it."

I contemplated the fact that if she and the deputy went to fisticuffs with each other, I'd have to step in and save my diminutive grandma. Just as I was planning how I might react if things went astray, the front door to the jail opened again and a large man stepped inside. His white felt Stetson made him appear bigger than life. His dark eyes flashed as he surveyed the situation before him.

"Good morning, Deputy!" The big man's tone was upbeat. "I'm Ranger Sam Judge, and I've come to assist Mrs. Roland with bringing these two gentlemen home."

I kept my mouth shut. So did Cowboy. Intuitively, we knew the best course of action was *no* action.

"Can you round up the paperwork so I can sign it?"

"Yes, sir." The deputy scurried to put his keys away. It was obvious he knew who Ranger Judge was, or at least knew his reputation. Shaking in his lizard boots, he said, "Ranger, I was just telling Mrs. Roland if she would vouch for these two not being vagrants then she would be free to walk out the front door with them right now." Even as he said the words, he stepped toward the open door behind the Ranger, pulling me and Cowboy alongside him. Then he used a sweeping gesture of his arm to usher us all through, while saying, "You folks have a nice day."

Cowboy and I went through first, followed by Nana Michelle. I stepped back to help her down the steps. She was much frailer than when I'd seen her this time last year. Ranger Judge came out last, but not before he said something to the deputy sheriff. I couldn't hear what it was, but I saw the deputy's already-pale face turn an even lighter shade.

* * *

Neither of us had a drop to drink; nevertheless I felt like I was suffering from a hangover. Cowboy didn't look much better.

I decided it would be best to let Nana Michelle do all the talking as we drove along. But she did very little talking, so we rode along in an awkward silence until Ranger Judge asked, "Where exactly does Johnny Whiskey live?"

Cowboy gave directions while I gazed in the truck's rearview. For the longest time, I could still see the deputy at the door, watching us as we drove away. My mind wandered as we bumped along the country road. Fields that used to be filled with flowing prairie grass now lay barren. What the drought didn't get, the grasshopper plagues or the jack-rabbit overpopulation did. Only a scant few drought-tolerant plants remained. For some reason, these made me think of Cowboy's father, living up there on the family farm and waiting for things to get better. He may have just been a hardscrabble farmer, but he was a survivor.

"Mick." The Ranger's voice woke me from my daydream. "I'm going to drop Cowboy off at Johnny Whiskey's place, but you'll have to go into town with me. You're a wanted man, even more so now that Clyde Barrow shot those highway patrolmen in cold blood."

Nana Michelle turned in the front seat and looked back at us. "Mick, those men at the jail might have taken 'wanted dead or alive' literally. I couldn't trust them to be rational after the horror that happened in Grapevine." She looked me over as if she was going to say something, but then thought better of it. After a moment, she continued, "Ranger Judge is going to help you out of this situation. You can't continue to run."

I decided to speak, at last. "Uncle Robert and Dad are trying to find some additional photos, to show I was *not* with Bud, but against him.

Maybe they can even get photos showing Bud holding a gun on me."

The Ranger cleared his throat. "Mick, the doctor called your grandmother to tell her your father and uncle went over to Cooper. But they hadn't had any more luck finding the school photographer than the investigator did. Seems the whole town has closed in around the man and won't give up his identity. Your mother called me direct and asked me to help."

"How do you know my mother!" I hadn't meant to raise my voice.

The Ranger didn't seem to notice. "Antonia and I go way back." He adjusted the rearview mirror to look at me. "Helped her out of a jam a long time ago. That's why she trusts me to do right by you now."

He sounded sincere, but my brain was running too fast. I rambled on in a high-pitched voice. "I can't believe they couldn't find the photographer." I was panicking. "I think he was the principal of the school. He should be easy to find."

"Apparently he isn't."

My heart was beating overtime as I realized I might not be able to prove my innocence. Slowing the truck, Ranger Judge pointed up ahead. He continued talking in his laid-back style. "Is Johnny Whiskey's house the one up the way?"

"Yessir," Cowboy answered.

My head hurt. My entire body hurt. If I didn't find a witness to the fact I didn't rob the filling station, then I'd be facing possible jail time —or possibly even death, if some vigilante decided he wanted justice.

"Sarah Michelle, you doing okay?" The Ranger addressed my Nana Michelle by her given name. His words jarred my memory. I had forgotten my Nana Michelle had heart problems.

"Fine." Her voice held none of the strength it had back at the jail cell. In fact, it wasn't even her usual voice. More of a squeaky whisper. I watched as she held a hand-embroidered handkerchief to her mouth. "It's the dust. So much gosh-darn dust."

* * *

Sitting in Dr. Dean's favorite chair at my grandparents' house, I took off my boots and put my socked feet up on the leather ottoman. I wondered how many times my grandfather might've taken a nap in this position. His leather-bound medical books in the bookshelves were free of dust, as if he might round the corner at any moment and pull one out for reference. The big table he used for a desk was polished to a high shine. I could still feel his presence in this room, though he'd died when I was a young boy.

I remember Nana Michelle sobbing while my father held her. For a while, she refused to eat or talk. My mother watched after her day and night, while sitters stayed with me and André. Katherine and Bobby weren't even born yet. To this day, they still ask me about Dr. Dean, or Pawpa as André and I used to call him. They really missed out not knowing him. He was a great man and a great doctor.

On the bookshelf I saw a family photo taken before I was born. Everyone in the picture was holding up a seashell. This was from the year the big house burned in Houston, just before the Christmas holiday. The gifts had been destroyed. But they had celebrated anyway, at the Hotel Galvez in Galveston. The only gifts anyone received that year were these seashells from the ocean. Nana Michelle said it was one of her favorite holidays; that was the year my mother and father were married in an impromptu wedding ceremony, on the hotel's balcony as they rang in the New Year.

It was hard to imagine life before I was born. So many things could've turned out differently. I might never have seen the light of day. I was grateful to be here, though my head still pounded like a drum and my throat burned from thirst. Still, this was much more comfortable than a Dalhart jail cell. The scent of the jail's peculiar cleaning agent lingered on my clothes. I smelled of lemon and urine at the same time. When I felt a bit better, I would take a bath. A hot one, with shampoo and lye soap.

Thank goodness, Ranger Judge had been kind enough to let me recover for the rest of the day before questioning me. I could hear the low rumble of his deep voice, talking on the kitchen telephone. Boy, was I glad he was on my side.

Nana Michelle had put a cup on the table beside me, medicated tea to help my migraine. I waited for it to cool. Drinking hot tea on a warm April day didn't seem like a great idea, but I didn't have the heart to tell her. I wished she'd brought iced tea instead. But Nana Michelle was born in London, and whenever she thought of tea, she thought of hot tea in a delicate cup.

I raised the bone china teacup to my lips. The tea soothed my thirst, and my thoughts turned to Margaret. Though she was a bit of a tomboy, I bet she'd think the teacup's rose pattern was pretty. I hoped she was getting back to the normal routine of her life. She was probably at school right now, eating lunch with her girlfriends.

Pulling up the pillow Nana Michelle had placed behind my back, I laid my head on it and curled on my side in the deep leather chair. Instinctively, my finger traced the metal studs framing the chair arm. I adjusted my long legs over the ottoman. Nana Michelle's hot tea was working. The headache eased, and I found myself drifting. In the background, I could still hear the Ranger working over the phone.

Half-asleep, I heard soft feet padding down the hall. Nana Michelle, checking on me. She didn't try to wake me, but instead pulled a blanket from a nearby closet and covered me with it. I smelled my grandfather's favorite cologne as she adjusted the cover around me.

She muffled a cough. I hoped she wasn't getting the dust

pneumonia that had killed so many.

MARGARET

Standing in front of the mirror in the Cooper school bathroom, I took the small cardboard box Doreen had given me out of my purse and powdered my nose with the puff. As I admired the gold and white toned flowers on the box lid, I noticed Samantha looking at me. "Haven't you ever seen face powder before?" I asked.

"Where on earth did you get it? And why are you putting it on now, before we go into meet with the principal about the photographs?"

"I want him to remember me. I had on lipstick and powder the day Bud robbed the filling station."

I got out the red lipstick and expertly applied it, as I had practiced over the last few weeks. Samantha's mouth fell open. She turned to her reflection in the mirror. "You look good. Now, let me try it."

* * *

Inside the principal's office, we sat on a wooden bench. I felt like we were waiting to be reprimanded. Samantha seemed upbeat as she looked through a plate glass window into the main foyer. Obviously, a lot of trophies had been won over the years.

Uncertainty and fear pounded in my chest. What if I was wrong and the principal wasn't the photographer? What would we say to him? Obviously, the townspeople wouldn't give up the photographer's identity to just anyone asking about him. But I knew what he looked like and I had taken care not to tell his secretary the true purpose of our visit. Before I could fret another second, the office door opened and a man entered, the same man who had taken the photographs. He didn't notice us at first.

Not until my sister spoke up and said, "My name is Samantha and this is my sister Margaret."

He gave a quick hop of surprise, recovered, and turned purposefully toward us. "What can I do for you? Are you new to the district?"

I spoke softly. "Sir, we're here to talk to you about the photographs from the day of the robbery."

He looked at me carefully. I saw recognition dawn in his eyes. "You're the girl that was talking in the parking lot with Bonnie Parker, aren't you? I snapped a good shot of you blowing the dandelion while she stood in the background, looking on. Didn't realize who she was at first. Little did I know I was about to capture the robbers' escape."

This was my chance to ask for the rest of the pictures. "Sir," I pleaded, "would it be possible for us to see the rest of the film you shot that day? The boy in one of the shots is in a lot of trouble, and he wasn't robbing the store. He was trying to *stop* the robber."

"So I've heard. Just about every person in town has been paid a visit by a private investigator this boy's parents hired to get him off scot-free, but I told everybody not to give out my name. Even had his father and uncle snooping around. They told people he was trying to stop the holdup, but I believe they're just trying to smooth the whole thing over and get their baby boy out of trouble. Didn't look to me like he was trying to stop anything." He put his hands on his hips and looked down at me in that intimidating way principals do. "It looked to me like they were fighting over the money. And you're part of their gang. I saw you hug Bonnie goodbye."

I looked from the principal to a very shocked Samantha. Her ruby lips fell open.

I hated to put the doctor and our parents' lives in jeopardy, but the truth needed to come out. If I told the truth, maybe people would understand why we helped the outlaws.

The principal towered over us. However, I could see a certain kindness in his eyes. Without hesitation I launched into the story of what happened that fateful day at the cabin on my parent's farm. To his credit, he heard me out without one interruption.

DR. JEROME LYLES

When Margaret and her sister called me to say they'd talked with the photographer and he'd given his additional photos to Ranger Judge, my relief was palpable. Mick would be exonerated. And Margaret and Samantha were safely home.

I had to admit, Margaret was one brave girl to go out on a limb and save a boy she'd just met. She was like her father, loyal through and through.

It looked like we'd all worried for nothing. The lawmen were not interested in arresting us for assisting two known outlaws. Rather, they understood the situation completely. They even mentioned more cases where Bud and Doreen had kidnapped citizens. They'd even kidnapped a police officer and let him go. I only hoped when the story of the kidnapping was printed with the additional photos, the public would be equally understanding.

We'd know in a day or two. Until then I needed to turn my attention to my patients. Mr. and Mrs. Chaney's new baby needed a one-month checkup. I'd stop by on my way to see the Newman's little pug, Sam.

I didn't usually care for dogs, but little Sam was like a child to them. When they'd begged me to take a look, I couldn't turn them down.

Perhaps I could do something to make their seventeen-year-old dog more comfortable, but I didn't have the proper medications for an animal. However, I could possibly get some kind of elixir from the feed store.

Olivia came into my office as I packed my medical bag. "I sterilized this scalpel Margaret brought back yesterday, when she and her sister dropped by to visit. Smart on your part to give it to her, considering the circumstances. But you should've known she wouldn't be able to hurt a soul."

"Don't underestimate Margaret." I took the shiny instrument from her. "She has a lot of verve—and so does our Mick. You'd have been proud of the way he tried to rescue us in the cabin with my gun."

Olivia sat beside me at the table as I packed my medical bag. "I told him not to take the gun. Said nothing good would come of it."

"Nothing good did come of it. In the end, the bad guy took it from him." I chuckled as I put my hand over Olivia's. "Now my favorite gun is probably his favorite gun."

My wife looked up at me with a serious expression. I stopped laughing, but I did give her a little smile. She didn't smile back.

"You could've all been killed. Did you read the reports about what those people did to the highway patrolmen? And last week they killed another lawman." She dabbed at the tears forming in her eyes. "Jerome, you could've died."

175

I pulled her close. "Now Olivia, I'm not going to die one moment before my time." I whispered the words as I swept back the soft hair framing her face. My dear wife had absolutely no idea how afraid I'd been that day.

If it was up to me, she never would.

* * *

It was a fine spring morning near the end of April, before the May showers begin and the summer weather gets hotter than Hades. I was enjoying the ride to the Chaney's house to check on their newborn. As I rounded the curve, I saw Rickey running down the dirt ruts that served as a drive.

"Dr. Lyles," he huffed as he came up to my open window. His hearty complexion was more flushed than usual. Recovering his breath, he continued. "I heard men talking in town. This morning's paper said you helped those bad people. Said you must've been in with their gang for them to call on you to take a bullet out." He braced one hand on the hood of my car and took another deep breath. "One of them said they were gathering a group to come get you."

Rickey started wheezing. His complexion glowed beet red. When he recovered a bit, he said, "We need to hide you. They're coming to get you."

"And what?" I said. "The police already know why I helped."

He went around and opened the passenger door. "My dad has a deer blind deep in the woods. I can hide you there."

"Rickey, it's okay."

"No, it's not, sir. They're bringing a noose. I saw one of 'em making it."

I didn't know what to do first, drive straight home to protect Olivia and the girls, or drive up to the Chaney's house and call the police.

Hopping in to ride shotgun, Rickey made the decision for me. "Let's go."

"I need to call the pol-"

"Dad's already called. Told me to take you to the deer blind."

"I can't put you in danger. I don't even have a gun to protect myself." *Or my girls*, I thought. "Rickey, I need to go to my family. It's too dangerous for them to face the men without me there."

"I'll go with you."

"Son, please get out. It's not safe."

"You need all the help you can get," he said.

I could see Rickey meant business. I gritted my teeth and headed back to my wife and daughters. The rough roads made for a jarring ride. Rickey braced himself on to the dash.

We were too late.

A small crowd, dressed in white sheets, had gathered outside my home. Not only did they have a noose, they were sitting up two pieces of timber wrapped in a white sheet. They were burning a cross in my front yard.

I tried to remain calm.

"Get down in the floorboard," I said. Rickey was a smart boy, I didn't have to tell him twice.

The flames licked the white sheet bound around the cross. The fire whipped high. My heart seized as I thought of my wife and girls.

As I got out of my truck and calmly closed the door behind me, the mob turned in my direction. I tried to walk confidently on my shaking legs. Fighting was not my forte—I was a doctor, not a warrior. I felt for the sterilized scalpel I had slipped in my doctor coat pocket and pricked my finger on its sharpness.

I yelled in a much stronger voice than I thought would come out. "What's this all about!" The sweat rolled off my brow. I could feel dampness under my arms, down my back. My mouth was dry and my vision blurred as I stepped up onto my porch. Before I could speak again, the wailing of a siren sounded in the distance. No one in the crowd said a word as it grew stronger. I stared at my neighbors. Though they were shrouded in white hoods, I knew I had saved some of their lives, and birthed their children.

"Sid, Lou," I called the names of two men whose lives I'd saved.

"Put the fire out, please. And no one here will get hurt today."

Two of the hooded figures set to work, and the flames were doused with water from my yard hose. Another siren screamed to life. The department had sent multiple cars, though it didn't look like they would be needed. Looking down at my white lab coat, I noticed a drop of blood on the pocket. Pulling my hand out, I released the scalpel I'd been holding in my fist. A small cut on my index finger bled a few drops.

The cut was small. But I'd carry this wound for the rest of my life.

7 PLAIN OLD ORDINARY SUFFERING

Happy, Texas

Tuesday Night

May 8, 1934

MICK

The clock on the fireplace mantel said five minutes till midnight, but I didn't feel the least bit tired. I needed to work out the song that kept running through my head. It had been far too long since I'd played, and my guitar was badly out of tune thanks to hopping boxcars. Miraculously, neither of us had dropped our cases too hard on any of those many occasions when we leapt out of train cars.

It had been silent in the room for the last few minutes, except for the ticking of the clock. I was looking forward to falling back to sleep.

That was when the melody came out of nowhere. It seemed to

arrive in my mind as if by destiny. I knew a person didn't have this sort of thing happen often in their life. In fact, I suspect some people never did. I knew instinctively it was necessary to get the song down on paper before it evaporated back into the fog from which it came.

The tune was unlike anything I'd heard before. It came hard and fast. My hand flew between my guitar strings and paper as I attempted to write it down perfectly the first time through. For this, I was glad my parents had insisted on only the best musical training. When I told my mother it wasn't necessary to learn to read notes, she'd said I needed to learn the correct way then I could play in any manner I wanted.

All the while I played, I had an image of Margaret's face on my mind. Clearly this song was for her. The ache that was deep in my soul spilled out through my fingertips. The crying guitar strings reflected the loneliness of being away from her . . . and the fear of her not returning my affection. Words were starting to come as well. It would only be a matter of time before the entire song took shape.

Without having to ask anybody, I knew it was good. I knew it was special.

Glancing over at the pile of dirty clothes Nana Michelle had said the maids would take care of tomorrow, I tried to keep my mind from wandering away from my songwriting. But it did, just for a moment. I looked down at the clothes she'd given me to wear. I knew they used to belong to my grandfather. Once again, the scent of his cologne washed over me. I felt him alongside me as I worked out the last of the melody and words. The shirt I was wearing—PawPa's shirt—was made of white cotton. I recognized it as being one of his favorites. Though it was well-made, it now was almost threadbare. His pants fit my tall, lanky frame loose and comfortable.

Everything was perfect. Everything was aligned.

A hot bath, clean clothes and a shave had removed the road grime that had clung to me for the last few weeks. I was so grateful Nana Michelle had been there for me when I needed her. She was the kind of person who knew how to take care of others—she instinctively knew what a person needed. This was what made her special.

I hoped my playing in the middle of the night didn't wake her.

* * *

The morning sun glittered through the split in the curtains. Slowly, I sat up in the feather bed in the guest room. My headache no longer plagued me.

Downstairs I could hear Nana Michelle and her cook Josie moving around in the kitchen. Even though they kept their voices low, they were betrayed by the occasional clink of dishes and glassware, and the sizzle of bacon frying in the pan.

Grabbing PawPa's clothes from the nearby chair, I dressed for the day. My clothes were being laundered, and I knew it would be late in the day before they dried. As I slipped down the back stairs near the kitchen, I heard Josie say, "The world's done gone wild. No wonder they refer to this decade as the Dirty Thirties. Economy tanking, crooks taking everything they can, young people breaking off from their families to ride the rails—"

"Now, Josie." Nana Michelle interrupted Josie's rant with her own. "I think maybe some of the young people riding the rails are trying to give their families a break from the responsibility of having so many young ones to care for. Some may be trying to find work to send money back home. Like that Cowboy Larson I met yesterday."

"That may be true." Josie expertly flipped bacon in the frying pan. "But I never thought I'd see the likes of these times. I guess you could be right. Some people are just doing what they can to get by. Trying to help others while bettering their own situation. Case in point, Pretty Boy Floyd. He's the outlaw who champions the poor. Heard some people call him 'Robin Hood of the Cookson Hills' because he shares the money from his robberies with them. Also, heard he tore up a bunch of mortgages at the last bank he robbed so the farmers wouldn't get their homes repossessed." Josie stopped talking and went back to cooking. Then she turned around and said, "Still, the world's gone crazy. Some of those outlaws, like John Dillinger, even making motion picture clips of themselves. You'd never have heard of something like that ten years ago."

Nana Michelle raised her head from the newspaper she was looking at and stared off into space. "Some say good things about the gangsters. But I suspect they're just basically bad to the core. There's no good reason to go around killing and stealing. Lots of folks affected by the bad times and they don't steal. Instead, they'd give you their last penny if you needed it. But I agree with you, Josie, it is bewildering."

As I turned the corner, Nana Michelle put down her newspaper and turned her attention on me. "Josie, look what the cat dragged in. It's my best grandson Mick." The morning sun showed up her many wrinkles, but her fine features still held their natural beauty. Her gentle personality shone through her twinkling eyes. PawPa was a lucky man to have known such love.

"You hungry, Mick?" The big cook started to make up plates, her weathered face shiny from slaving over the hot stove. But she spoke in a jovial tone. "I've got bacon, eggs, and oatmeal." She wiped her hands on her stark white apron without leaving a mark.

"I'll just take orange juice, thank you," I said. My stomach rumbled.

"Your belly says otherwise." Josie put a heaping plate of steaming food on the table and pushed me toward the chair in front of it. "Don't go hurtin' my tender feelings by turning down my cooking."

I doubted if Josie had tender feelings, but I didn't dare say this out loud. So I sat down in the hardback chair she'd indicated. After all, her cooking did smell delicious. I thought back to my recent travels on the empty boxcars and how hungry I'd gotten. Up until just a few weeks ago, I'd never experienced hunger or depravity of any kind. I had no frame of reference for it even though I did empathize with those in need. But I'd never really understood. I guess I thought maybe people who were in a bad spot financially just needed to work harder. However, if I wanted to be honest with myself, the truth was I'd never thought much about it. I didn't even realize I'd had an entitled attitude. Didn't even know what it was called until Cowboy brought it up. Seems he'd had an entitled attitude too until the drought ended his father's wealth abruptly.

Nana Michelle spread out the newspaper so I could see too. It wasn't today's paper, it was the paper from a few days ago. The one where Margaret and the principal told our true story.

"Mick, I thought I'd keep this particular newspaper for your scrapbook." Nana Michelle gave a wry smile and her eyes twinkled.

"Actually, I did want to read the story." I replied with a little smirk. I sipped on my juice.

"It's a good one," Josie said over her shoulder as she buttered biscuits at the stove. "You owe that Margaret Morningstar. That girl saved your life. I hope it don't come back to haunt her parents and the doctor who helped the gangsters. Seems like most people would understand why they helped under the circumstances, but these are crazy times . . . people want those two fugitives dead. Especially after what happened on Easter Sunday. Killing those two young highway patrolmen in cold blood like that—the one trooper only twenty-six years old with a young wife of two years. The other'n twenty-two and fixin' to get married. It's a downright shame, it is. Heard they shot and killed Constable Campbell just a week later and abducted a Police Chief." Josie pounded her fist on the old oak table, making our plates rattle. "It is time, I tell you, it is time to rid the world of these hard-hearted gangsters."

"Now Josie," Nana Michelle said, looking at my horrified face. "It hasn't been proven Bonnie and Clyde shot those men. Some believe another gang member who was riding along with them did it."

Josie's words were harsh. I thought back to the two outlaws who had kidnapped us, about their personalities. I found it hard to believe Bonnie could shoot someone in such a merciless manner. Clyde, maybe. He was certainly capable of murder.

I thought back to how his temper could turn on a dime, how I too had almost been shot by him. Even though the morning was warming the already hot kitchen even more, my blood ran cold, and I stood to go look out the screened back door to try to shake the feeling.

"I don't care," Josie said behind me. A touch of anger laced her voice. "It's a turning point for those two outlaws. The public is no longer romanticizing them. . . . They want them dead." As if to emphasize the point, she all but threw the knife she was using in the sink full of soapy water.

I took a deep breath. Seemed like the hard times were bringing out the best and worst in people. Josie spoke for half the country, but I understood her position on the subject.

No one said anything for a good while. Then out of nowhere Nana Michelle said, "Mick, that was a right pretty song you were playing last night. Did you make it up?"

"Yes, ma'am. I did."

"You've a special gift for music, like the other music people on your daddy's side. Music is in your genes."

Nana Michelle didn't say who she was referring to, but I knew she'd adopted my father as an infant after the Great Hurricane of 1900. My father knew some about his real mother, but he never spoke about it. Told me once he'd talk to me about it when I was older. I never asked him for more information because I wasn't sure I wanted to know.

Just like Bonnie and Clyde's families, our family had some black sheep of its own. I hoped I wasn't going to accidentally be another one of them. I vowed to be more careful of my actions from this point onward. I thought back to the day I went to the worker's cabin, trying to help the doctor. Once again, my mind played out the scenario in every way possible, searching for a better outcome. Even if I had gone to get the Sheriff, Bud might've killed everyone in the cabin before he surrendered.

* * *

The phone rang. I jumped like a horn toad being chased by a coyote. Nana Michelle had an extra-loud ringer because PawPa was almost deaf. But now that he'd been gone upwards of seven years, she still hadn't brought it back down to a normal level. Maybe because she too was losing her hearing. She said she kept the ringer at blasting-eardrum level because it reminded her of the old coot—and so she could hear it as far as the barn. She could probably hear it in the next county, I figured.

After a brief hello to the person on the other end, Nana Michelle handed the receiver to me. It was Cowboy. He'd landed a gig for us up near Dallas, which meant we'd need to leave West Texas no later than the thirteenth if we wanted to make it there on time. My heart jumped when I realized it was already close to that date.

I listened as he detailed out a plan to hop a train.

Though she pretended to be doing embroidery, I knew Nana Michelle was eavesdropping. Apparently her hearing was excellent because she said, "How about you boys use your grandfather's fancy automobile instead of riding the rails?" She broke a thread with her teeth before adding, "I've had my mechanic keep it in top-notch condition so Josie can drive me to town. Might keep you out of jail."

Just like that, she offered up grandfather's favorite thing in the world as if it wasn't special to her. As much as I wanted, I didn't feel I could take her up on her offer.

Then to my surprise Cowboy said from the other end of the phone. "An automobile would be safer for our guitars."

I wanted to hand the phone to Nana Michelle and say, *I'll just let you two talk*. But I didn't. For once, I truly appreciated my family's wealth —especially after seeing how so many others were suffering through no fault of their own. I winced as I thought of how many things I'd taken for granted. But how was I to know any different?

Cowboy went on to ask if he could bring his girl Saint on the trip down south. She'd been living at the Boarding School all year and she wanted to visit relatives for the summer. This would be her only chance for a ride to Dallas. If we didn't take her with us, she'd have to stay and work at the restaurant near the school for the next few months.

"Of course," I heard myself say. The thought of Cowboy bringing his girlfriend made my thoughts turn once again to Margaret. I missed her so. Maybe I'd get to see her in Dallas.

But, she hadn't answered the letter I sent her.

DR. JEROME LYLES

Outside the church, newspaper photographers hovered with flash cameras strung around their necks, waiting to get a picture at a moment's notice. Pushing my fedora down over my eyes, I drove around the corner and parked. I headed toward the side entrance on the south side of the building, an unassuming entrance that few parishioners even knew was there. Carefully, silently, I opened the side door to the auditorium and slipped inside. Immediately, I felt the entire congregation turn to look at me. Taking off my hat, I surveyed the pews for an empty space where I could take a seat and disappear.

Taking a few steps forward, I looked to my right, where my family was seated on a pew down front. Olivia sat with both girls beside her. Heads held high. Backs ramrod straight. All three had wanted me to enter the sanctuary with them, but I'd told Olivia I'd make less disturbance if I slipped into the back entrance during the start of the service. Obviously, my plan hadn't worked. I couldn't believe the reaction from the congregation. My feet felt like they were slugging through mud as I made my way down the carpeted aisle.

Now that it was known I'd saved an outlaw's life, my life was no longer my own. People made judgements about me without examining the facts. They didn't know my motivation, yet they made assumptions about my private life to suit their own agendas. There was no way to stop the trail of gossip spreading across the community, and maybe even the country. The rumors that hurt me the most were the ones claiming I was taking big payments in exchange for attending to the medical needs of gangsters. My practice was already suffering, and it'd only been a few days since the rumor mill opened for business. A third of my patients had canceled appointments. The phone no longer rang off the wall. However, I knew deep down there was no stopping the lies against my character; these I would endure until—hopefully—I came out on the other side.

I looked up at the pulpit. True to his composed nature, the pastor kept preaching even though he knew people were no longer listening. His baritone vibrated as he accented his words with his mighty fist on the hard oak in front of him.

Suddenly he stopped mid-sentence and turned his attention my way. I could feel all eyes on me.

The pastor's voice softened. "Doctor Lyles. As a physician, you have saved many lives, have you not?"

I answered simply. "Yessir, I have." My eyes glanced over the crowd. My friends, my neighbors. Their faces showed utter contempt.

The pastor's voice grew louder. "Dr. Lyles, you were put on this earth to save lives, were you not?"

I looked at the pulpit. My gaze met his. "It was my calling," I said.

191

"Then I will not question your actions. I will leave judgment to the Lord. And I suggest everyone else do the same. This congregation has known you for many years, and you've helped all of us at some point, in one way or another. No, I will not question you, rather I will stand behind you. I trust you to always do that which is right, even if it might seem wrong at first glance, for I know your heart is in the right place."

He gestured with his open hand toward Olivia, who had tears in her eyes. "Now, come sit with your wife and family. You are a child of God, and you'll be recognized as such by your church family."

The hatred and tension in the room faded. I released the breath I'd been holding. Olivia beckoned me to sit beside her.

As I moved to take my place on the pew, the congregation spontaneously burst into applause. There were still a few people in the world who believed in me, who loved me unconditionally.

MARGARET

As I walked home from school, strolling down the tree-lined road
to our house, I contemplated my situation. Even though I'd heard Dr.
Lyles had a cross burnt on his front lawn, I hadn't expected there to be
any trouble for me helping the outlaws. After all, I was just a schoolgirl.
But today had gone bad for me.

I'd gotten up at the crack of dawn to get all pretty for a retake of
our school picture. Seems I wasn't the only one who missed the first one
back in late March. The Dawson twins had had the chicken pox and Linda
Grayson had been out of town for her grandmother's funeral. But the real
reason the photo was being retaken, I suspected, was that our teacher Mrs.
Ross had her eyes closed and her mouth contorted in the first photo.
She'd been yelling at students to be quiet at the instant the photo was
snapped.

Of course, on that day, I'd been on the road with Bud, Doreen,
and Mick. But I'd heard how funny her face looked in the photo, and I
had every reason to believe what my classmates said was true. Absolutely
everybody was whispering about the funny picture. And apparently, a few
were whispering bad things about me.

As I entered the ladies' room near the gym, I saw Cindy and
Mildred whispering into each other's ears. I went to the mirror over the

sink and leaned forward to check my makeup. Having added a little color to my face, I stepped back to adjust my ribbon.

But Cindy was faster.

"Let me get that for you." She jerked the ribbon off my head, taking a few strands of hair with it.

Mildred shoved me up against the tile wall. Her hot breath puffed against my cheek. "You look like a hussy with that paint on your face." I could smell the bacon she'd eaten for breakfast and it made me nauseous. Shoving her fleshy body away, I escaped her grasp as she fell against one of the stall doors.

Clinging tightly to my purse, I tried to get my sister's good ribbon back from Cindy. But she turned on the faucet and put the satin ribbon under the running water. I snatched it back but had to wad it up in my hand to keep it from her. Then, my closed hand turned into a balled fist. I was punching her. When her nose began to bleed, I stopped.

I turned my attention to Mildred, caught her slipping out the wooden ladies' room door. As she held the door open, I saw the "Women Only" sign behind her head. I almost halted my unladylike behavior. Then I looked down at the one piece of finery I owned—and realized I didn't even own it, my sister did.

I jumped on Mildred's back and put my arm around her neck, pulling and pulling at her hair. She screamed for mercy. No one came.

Behind me, Cindy cowered in the corner.

Finally, with what I thought was a great deal of dignity, I released the crying girl. Mildred slumped to the floor, and I stood with my head held high, not unlike I'd seen Doreen do back at the filling station just before they released us. In some ways, Doreen had become my role model. We were both fighters, both survivors. Good people who'd been pushed too far.

Trembling, Cindy came forward to help her friend Mildred. But she must've seen the burning anger in my eyes because she backed off.

With one last look in the mirror, I combed my hair into place with my fingers before dropping the mangled ribbon in my purse and snapping it shut. Stepping over Cindy and Mildred, I went out to the hallway and followed the rest of the class to the gym auditorium. After all, I told myself as I wiped a bit of blood off my hand with my dark skirt, I didn't want to miss this photo retake. It'd be a memory to cherish.

* * *

I arrived at the side of our house. Mollie Belle ran from the chicken coop to meet me, her tail wagging, her eyes bright. At least someone still loved me.

I bent to rub her blue-gray fur. She was a good farm dog and a good guard dog. Usually she met me at the gate, but today she was distracted by my little brother. The two of them were chasing chickens around the coop, looking for tonight's dinner. As I passed by, he tried to explain to me how to snap a chicken's neck. "Really," I told him. "I don't want to know. Let me go inside for a cool drink."

As I put my hand on the screen door, my sister appeared. Anxiety overcame me as I thought of the ribbon she'd given me, now wadded up in my purse and unfit to be used again.

"Margaret Rebecca," she said. "I know about your little altercation in the ladies' room."

"You do?" Was she psychic?

"Everybody does," my brother chimed in. He and Mollie Belle had snuck up behind me. "Our school ain't that big, a story like yours goes round faster than lightning."

I looked defiantly up at Samantha. "Am I in trouble?"

"No." She reached out to stroke my cheek like our mother used to do when we were little. "Let's just say everyone knows not to mess with Margaret Morningstar."

"Ain't that the truth." My little brother brushed past me to go inside, holding his hands up in a sign of surrender.

I felt an uneasiness in my heart.

MICK

When I entered the front room, I found Nana Michelle sitting close to the radio with a concerned look on her face. Josie stood nearby, wiping her hands on her apron, mumbling: "Oh, dear, oh, dear."

"What is it?" I asked.

Josie twisted the crisp white material in her hands. "A dust storm like no other is sweeping through the Great Plains. The brunt of it might be headed our way."

I turned to Nana Michelle, who stared calmly out the window. "Mick," she said. "Help me lock the windows. Josie, alert the farm hands to get as many animals as possible inside. Tell them to board up the barns and the chicken coop, so the animals have a chance."

"Is there going to be time for all that?" I asked. The skies were already darkening.

"I don't know." Nana Michelle rose from her seat and began shutting the window nearest her. "Josie, tell them to do what they can but not to risk their own lives."

Josie ran out. Soon we heard her screaming, "Dust storm! Dust storm!" Her voice caught in the rising wind as I shut window after window at the front of the house.

"It'll be sweltering inside if we close everything," I said, pushing down hard on a stuck frame. "The animals won't survive the heat inside the closed barn."

"They might not make it outside in the dust storm either," Nana Michelle replied.

The door blasted open and Josie appeared, her face red from exertion. Her tightly braided bun was coming loose, and her pristine apron had dirt marks. "I need one of those silver pans I use for the laundry." Her words came out punctuated by short gasps. "The workers are going to put extra water in the barn for the animals."

She ran through the house toward the back stoop, calling back over her shoulder. "The lead foreman has started bringing in horses and goats. The men are trying to round up the cattle. Hopefully, most of them are grazing nearby."

Sweating profusely, I raced around slamming windows and doors. The house was built with rows of windows to assist the airflow through its spacious rooms and two main hallways. With the aid of the West Texas wind, this usually kept the place pleasant inside, especially throughout the rooms on the bottom floor. However, the windows were hardly ever shut unless a severe thunder storm blew up. During those rare times, it was usually the servants who closed and locked them. But at this moment only the two of us were left to do the task. Annette, the cook, was on vacation with her daughter over in Lubbock, and Josie was outside helping the men with the animals. For once in my life, I wished Nana Michelle staffed her house fully like my father and Uncle Robert did. At this moment, I'd have been happy to have a plethora of help falling all over the place. Still, Grandmother looked cool as a cucumber as she moved along the southern side of the room. I wondered how she found the strength in her frail hands to get the windows down.

Josie came rushing back through with the big laundry pan, throwing wet tea towels in our direction. Quick as a flash, I brought my hand up to catch one. Nana Michelle's reflexes weren't quite as fast and hers fell to the floor. She bent to pick up the soaked rag before stuffing it in her dress pocket, where it made a wet spot on her floral dress.

"Good thinking!" Nana Michelle called out. But Josie had already raced outside. Nana Michelle turned to me. "The men are going to need soaked towels to breathe through as the silt starts rolling. I know from experience, wet material is the only thing that makes it possible to breathe in the dust clouds."

As I took the servant's stairs on the side of the house up to the second floor, I called down. "You really think the dust will come our direction?"

"Best be prepared." Nana Michelle hollered back. "We'll laugh about it later, if all our hard work comes to naught."

On the second floor, I stopped at a window and watched Josie chasing a chicken across the front lawn with a broom. Near the barn, workers were bringing in animals two at a time not unlike Noah's ark. The foreman strung a line of new rope from the barn all the way to the side door of the house by the kitchen.

"Let's just hope this dust storm doesn't last long." Nana Michelle said from downstairs as the sky darkened overhead. "The newsmen are always exaggerating things. This should blow over in no time."

Back downstairs, I found Nana Michelle in the front room looking through the plate-glass window toward the barn. Dirt was descending like a darkened thundercloud, blocking out the noonday sun. I could see Josie holding one of the farm dog's puppies in her arms. The mother dog ran beside her. Josie's apron had become a ragged mess. When they reached the barn, the door slid open and a hand pulled her inside. The mother dog followed behind, almost tripping Josie.

"Good," Nana Michelle said. "Everyone is safely inside. Except I'm uncertain about Maxie, the new hand from Fort Worth. He's good with horses and cattle, but I'm not certain he knows how to ride out a dust storm. It'd just be a matter of luck if he survived outdoors." She never turned her face from the window as she spoke. "I just wish I'd seen Maxie go into the barn. Then I'd feel better."

I made my way around the dark room to the radio.

"Electricity is out," Nana Michelle said. She held her wet tea towel up to her mouth.

"Of course." I looked around for my tea towel.

"Yours is in the kitchen, on the table where you left it."

I ran to the kitchen to get it, with Nana Michelle following at her own pace. The wind screamed as it flung sticks and pebbles against the wooden exterior. Through the paned windows, I could just see dirt being tossed against the glass as if someone were out there flinging shovelfuls at us.

Nana Michelle put her ear against the side door. I went and stood beside her. Outside, a cow mooed in distress. Someone—or something— pounded against the door. Nana Michelle jumped back but quickly recovered and undid the locks.

"What are you doing?" I asked. "We can't let a cow inside."

"Yes, we can."

She cracked open the door, and silt spilled in over the pristine kitchen floor. A cow's head pushed its way inside, its brown eyes rolling wildly. The animal barged through the opening, pushing Nana Michelle out of its way. As I shoved the door closed behind the animal, I heard another sound. A man's dry voice, crying for help. Barely more than a whisper.

Beside my left foot, through the cracked door, I saw the gloved hand of a cattleman. I opened the door, and detected a patch of auburn hair amid the swirling dirt. It was Maxie. He'd fallen down on the side porch and the dust had already covered him.

I dragged him inside, using the doorframe to steady myself. He was a big man and he tried to help, but he was having trouble. He clawed and crawled the best he could.

Finally, he was in far enough for me to shut the door behind him. It took all my might to get it closed tight against the unrelenting wind.

I looked down at Maxie. A gash in the back of his left calf shone bright red against the dirt all over his body. Even his curly red hair and ears were full of silt.

He scraped mud from his mouth and tongue with two dirt-covered fingers. Quickly, I gave him my wet towel.

I remembered Josie talking about how losing the topsoil to the wind was going to set this area back for years when it came to growing crops. But there was no time to think about that, I needed to help this man somehow—and I needed to round up the cow.

The cow! "Where'd the cow go?" I yelled to no one in particular, as the winds reached a fevered pitch on the other side of the door.

"I don't know," Maxie wheezed. "I lost hold of her lead rope when the pitchfork was blown against my leg." He used my soaked tea towel to remove the remaining mud from his tongue. "The dang cow was so scared it bucked away from me," he sputtered. That's when I realized she was kicking against something solid. I knew then we were at the house. I'd seen the foreman stringing the rope between the structures earlier. Can't believe I was able to follow it right up to the porch. Course, I thought I was headed toward the barn."

"Here," I said to Maxie as I poured him a glass of water from the pitcher on the counter.

A soft moo came from the hallway outside the kitchen.

Poking my head out, I found Nana Michelle gently stroking the cow's nose as she held the lead rope around its neck with her other hand. "There, there old girl," she said. The cow snorted dust from its nostrils.

I was speechless. There stood my grandmother, on her priceless oriental rug beside her fine china cabinet, snuggling a giant milk cow. I remembered her telling us grandkids, "Things don't matter, people do." Apparently, this life philosophy extended to livestock.

"Mick," she said as if it were any other normal day. "Fetch your grandfather's medical kit from his office closet. Looks like I'm going to be teaching you how to sew up a leg wound today. Also, pick up a bottle of whiskey from his bar, if you will. If you can't find whiskey, vodka will do."

* * *

As the demon winds swirled around the wooden farmhouse that'd kept my grandparents and father safe for so many years, I let the fear flow from me. Maybe it was the sip of whiskey I'd stolen, or maybe it was my grandmother's serene demeanor. But somehow, I gained confidence as we prepared Maxie's leg for surgery.

The wound gaped. Grandmother gave our patient more than a few sips of whiskey before we began. She told him she didn't want to use ether, as he'd gotten so much dust in his throat and lungs.

"Maxie"—her voice was almost jolly—"you're in luck. Not everyone has a complete operating room in their house. My husband would be proud to know it's being put to good use today."

I moved in closer with the oil lamp so Nana Michelle could get a good look at the back of his calf. Even though we'd cleaned it thoroughly, it was still a bloody mess just above his ankle. But grandmother seemed to think it was salvageable so I kept my mouth shut. "No major muscles or tendons severed," she said.

She considered the situation for a moment. Moving up towards Maxie's head, she said, "You might want to take another drink. This is going to sting."

He took a big swig.

Without warning, grandmother picked up a bottle of rubbing alcohol and poured it over the wound, covering every inch of his calf. When she finished, Maxie's face was as red as his hair. "Feel free to curse," she said. "I know it burns like hellfire."

Maxie didn't curse, just bit down on his pillow.

Preparing to stitch his leg wound, Nana Michelle motioned for me to come closer to the operating table. "Try not to kick out," she said to Maxie. "I've got the oil lamp situated near your leg so I can see."

Her thin fingers made precise even movements as she laced the skin back together. In the corner of the room, the old milk cow shuffled her feet.

Maxie had told me her name was Lucy. Said she was one of his favorites. Apparently she was a favorite of grandmother's too because she'd insisted on bringing the animal into the doctor's office with us. Said the cow would be less frightened staying with the group and therefore would get in less trouble. I wondered what was going through Lucy's bovine brain. She didn't seem to be bothered by the fact she'd found herself inside the main house instead of the barn with the herd.

"Mick," Nana Michelle explained, "Stitch like this if you want to leave a nice-looking scar."

"Yes," Maxie grunted, "a good-looking scar is important to me."

I had to laugh that he could even talk given all he'd been through. His words were slurred. The whiskey was doing its job.

Grandmother handed me the needle to finish the last half-inch. "Okay, now you."

I'd wondered why she also poured alcohol over my hands. Our hands had dried quickly, but I wasn't sure if mine were still sterile.

She pulled me to where she was standing. Holding the needle and catgut thread, my fingers felt big and clumsy. I'd watched her work, but I didn't dream she'd want me to take over.

"You learn best by doing," she said. "Use a light touch."

If Maxie was worried, he didn't let on. I worked as fast as I could to finish up the last inch or so. When we finished, Nana Michelle cleaned the wound with alcohol again, using cotton pads to get up all the blood. She expertly bandaged the leg, from the knee to the ankle. I stood by, holding the lamp.

Looking up, I was shocked to see Lucy had moved closer behind us and was nudging grandmother on the back with her nose. "There, there old girl," Nana Michelle said as she backed up past the cow. Going to the cabinet, she put the leftover bandage and rubbing alcohol away. Then she pulled a rolling metal stool over to the patient's table and sat down. Her lips were blue again. Reaching out to take her hands, I felt her trembling.

"You've got the hands of a surgeon," she said. "Strong and steady, with long fingers. Good for holding a scalpel or a needle." She thought for a second. "Also good for playing a guitar, I guess. Only you know what you were put on this earth to do. Can't none of the rest of us decide for you."

Maxie took another nip of whiskey. "Thank you both," he said, closing his eyes.

Grandmother patted him on his upper back. "We'll get you a full bath when this storm is over. Then you'll feel like a million dollars."

Maxie didn't hear grandmother. He was already softly snoring.

* * *

As the kettle heated up on the old gas cookstove, I searched the pantry and found a box of Earl Grey tea bags. I put it on the counter and got down a teacup.

"Use the good china," Nana Michelle said from her place at the kitchen table. Lucy was in the washroom at the back of the house, just a few steps away. I had talked grandmother into putting her there, as her hooves were leaving dents on the kitchen linoleum. Over by the door was a dust pile as high as my shin, where Maxie had entered. I remembered how the wind had driven the gritty particles into my skin as I attempted to drag him inside. How it boiled over in rolling clouds, forcing itself through the doorway like a monster. I couldn't imagine what kind of torture being outside had been for Maxie and Lucy. Thank goodness the foreman had tied the rope up for a guideline between the house and barn. It had literally saved Maxie's life. And Maxie had saved Lucy's. I wished I could say I'd have done the same for the cow, but I didn't know that I would.

I wasn't the hero type. I was more of an "I'll-help-you-if-it-doesn't-hurt-me" kind of person, and for that I hated myself. Who knew, maybe Lucy had saved Maxie's life when she kicked at our side door. Still, he had held her lead rope and tried to bring her to safety.

The cow snorted in the washroom. Probably thirsty.

As if reading my mind, Nana Michelle got out a large bowl and handed it to me. I filled it with water from the sink. "Can a cow eat uncooked oatmeal?" I asked over the rushing water.

"Let's mix it with water to aid her digestion. I can't think of anything else to feed her. She's already on the skinny side because of the drought."

I poured oats into another bowl. "How long do you think this dust storm will last?"

Grandmother didn't answer my question. Instead she went to the whistling tea kettle and poured hot boiling water into one of her finest teacups. I knew the china had come all the way from England, the place of her birth. Despite its fragility, it had survived the Great Galveston Hurricane she and granddad had ridden out years ago. Finally, as she put an Earl Grey teabag into the boiling water, she responded. "The question is not how long it will last, but how we can entertain ourselves while we wait it out. I absolutely can't believe it has raged on for so long."

I carried the metal bowls filled with water and oats to the washroom, suggesting over my shoulder that we play cards.

"That's what your grandfather and his friends did during the hurricane."

I stuck my head back around the washroom door. "He played cards during a hurricane?"

"Yes. He played poker with his friends."

"I think maybe you need to tell me more about PawPa," I said. "He sounds like my kind of guy." I placed the food and water near Lucy's head and, I swear, before she began to eat, the old cow looked up at me with gratitude in her eyes. I felt a stab of guilt that I'd wanted to push her back outside into the storm. "Everybody eats," I said to her, patting her back gently. It was a saying I'd heard my own father use again and again.

Going back to sit at the kitchen table with grandmother, I could almost imagine all was right with the world—except for the fact we had a cow in the house.

"How you holding up, boy?" Nana Michelle asked.

"Fine," I said. "Was just thinking how I hope my dad goes ahead and runs for office now that Margaret and the photographer set everything right about me in the newspapers."

Grandmother put down her cup of tea and picked up a spoon to stir it. She looked off toward the hallway. "Mick, I wasn't going to tell you, but I think you need to know, what with you and Cowboy headed back to Dallas in a few days."

I felt a sharp bite of panic in my gut as she continued.

"Some men burned a cross in Dr. Lyles's yard. Said they thought he was a doctor for the gangsters and that's how he's making all his money. Said they wanted to see him hang for keeping a wanted fugitive alive."

A cold feeling crept over me. I'd never thought of what would happen if people knew Dr. Lyles had saved Doreen. How they wouldn't know he did it with a gun trained on him.

Grandmother watched my face. "Ever since those patrolmen were shot, tensions have been running high. People want the criminals, dead or alive. And they're not thinking too clearly as to who they punish. They want justice of any kind."

"What's going to happen to Dr. Lyles? And his family?"

"I talked to him on the phone before the storm. He says his real friends are standing by him, but it has cost him his reputation with a lot of folks."

We sat silent. Then Nana Michelle said, "Even as a little boy sitting at this very table, Jerome dreamed of being a doctor like your grandfather. He studied hard to achieve that goal. Jerome was one of those people who always cared about how others perceived him. He always tried his best at everything he did. Being ostracized is killing him more than any gunshot."

I thought back to the day Margaret came flying on her horse to ask Dr. Lyles for help. She'd let him know the facts, and he'd made his own decision about helping. *No one is going to think less of you for not coming.* Margaret's exact words. The doctor had not hesitated. He came to her family's and Doreen's rescue. I remembered him saying to his wife as he kissed her goodbye that he'd taken an oath to save lives.

Now, he'd pay for his good deed for the rest of his life.

Grandmother broke my reverie as she stood and went to the window. "There seems to be a break in the storm."

I went to stand beside her. That's when we saw the foreman slide out of the barn door. Fighting the wind, he made his way toward us by holding to the rope as a guide. At times, the force of the wind drove him to his knees. His bandana was tied over his nose, and he held his hat against the side of his face to protect him from the driving dirt particles.

I opened the side door as he got to the porch. Reaching out my hand, I pulled him inside and slammed the door shut. With his hands on his knees, he tried to catch his breath.

"Maxie is unaccounted for," he said.

Nana Michelle pointed down the hallway. "Maxie's here, resting in the other room. He hurt his leg."

The foreman let out a sigh of relief. I went to pour him a glass of water and he took it with a nod of thanks. In the next room, Lucy shuffled and snorted.

"And Lucy is in the washroom," grandmother said.

The foreman's eyes shot a surprised look in my direction, but his face remained unfazed. I took it the man had seen a lot in his life, especially working for Nana Michelle. "Ma'am," he said. "I need to get food to my men, and get Josie back to the house now the storm's dying down a little. It's been going nigh near twenty-two hours, and it looks like the hard part is over. But you never know, it could start back up again. I've never seen anything like it."

Nana Michelle and I had been up all night. I must have been running on adrenaline because it only felt like a few hours. Glancing over at grandmother, I realized she must be beyond exhausted. For the first time, I understood the superhuman strength in her tiny frame. "I don't like to carry burdens," she'd said once. "I like to sit them down and let the Lord take care of them." At the time, I'd wondered what she meant. Now that I'd observed her grace under pressure, I knew.

"Mick," she said with heavy-lidded eyes. "Will you check on Maxie while we scare up something for the men and Josie to eat? Ask him if he's ready for breakfast." She started to cough from deep in her chest. "Go on now," she said, "this isn't the first dust storm I've weathered, living out on the High Plains."

8 SOMETHING OUT OF NOTHING

MARGARET

Dr. Lyles's daughter, Jenny Leigh, was picking her way across the open field between our family's properties. The cockleburs were out this season, and she had to be extra careful as she wore sandals. In her left hand she carried something paperish and white. My heart leapt at the prospect of a letter.

Putting down the chicken-feed pail, I wiped my hands on my apron and straightened my hair. "Jenny Leigh," I called. "How are you?"

She waved and walked faster, but I couldn't wait. I started in her direction, trying not to run. We met beside the big oak tree.

"This is for you." She placed an envelope in my hand. "Mick didn't know your address so he sent it to me and asked me to hand deliver it." The stationery was high quality, and the letter had some weight to it. The stamp was from well over a week ago.

"Sorry I'm so late." She twisted one foot behind her. "I'm sure you heard about the men and the burning—" She raised her head, looking off into the distance as if not wanting to relive the nightmare. "Anyway, Daddy and Mama wouldn't let me out of their sight after that incident. Said he'd drop this letter by to you, but he got busy with work. It's not like him to forget."

Holding the envelope toward the sun, I could see the writing inside.

"That's understandable," I said. "Perhaps I should walk you home."

"You don't have—"

"I want to." I thought of how I'd been innocently walking home from school when this whole mess started. One could never know the dangers lurking outside the front door. I would never be so nonchalant about a casual encounter again.

As we walked, the sun warmed me to the core. Butterflies danced across a sprinkling of wild flowers, and the wind rushed over the tall grass in soft gusts, creating a rippling effect. A beautiful Texas day—at least on this side of the state. I thought of the cloud of dust storms that had raged through the plains in the last few days, headed east. It was all the radio newsmen could talk about. One of them said the silt and sand had blown as far as New York and Atlanta on the East Coast. Ships three hundred miles offshore in the Atlantic had dust collect on their decks. One ship had as much as a quarter inch of soil on its deck. When I told Jenny Leigh as much, she turned her intelligent eyes to me. "Do you think that's true, Margaret?"

I told her a newsman had reported it and the radio reporters must have rules about getting the facts correct. She nodded her head in agreement. She hesitated before continuing. "My daddy says to question everything."

"Your daddy is a wise man."

Flipping the letter, I looked at the return address. Dalhart, Texas. I hoped Cowboy and Mick were safe. They must've had a heck of a time weathering the dust storms. The thick clouds of silt stretched from horizon to horizon, totally blotting out the sun—no one in their path could escape them. They'd have to bunker down in a shelter and ride it out. My heart twisted with worry. Surely someone out west would've notified Dr. Lyles and Mick's family if things weren't okay with him and Cowboy.

Guessing what was on my mind, Jenny Leigh touched my arm. "Mick's going to be okay. He's one of those people that always comes out on top." She tilted her head and gave me a little smile. "Not unlike you,

Margaret."

"What do you mean?"

She giggled. "I heard about your big fight the other day. Everybody has." Changing the subject, the young girl said, "I'm almost home. Why don't you run on back and read Mick's letter? I can tell you're busting at the seams to open it."

MICK

A girl who must've been Cowboy's girlfriend was sitting in the front seat of Johnny Whiskey's old truck, on the passenger side. Cowboy was squished in the middle, and Johnny himself was behind the wheel. I was glad to see them pull up on the gravel drive in front of grandmother's house. We needed to hit the road. As it was, we were already going to be a few days late to our Dallas gig because of the dust storm. But the owner of the club had told us to come on anyway.

The girl's dark eyes followed me as I approached the truck. She didn't turn her face to me so much as she watched me from the corner of her eye, with her face straight ahead. She made no acknowledgment of my presence.

Cowboy had told me her name was Saint, and, I had to say, the name seemed to fit. With tightly braided hair wrapped in a fashionable coil, her high-collared cotton dress set off her high cheek bones to perfection. A Cameo brooch shone from her neck. In her hand, she held a lace fan and a shell-colored clutch. If she hadn't been sitting in an old pickup truck on a cattle ranch in West Texas, I might've guessed she was a princess.

I opened the door for her, but she still didn't acknowledge me. Instead she looked down. I felt like a servant who shouldn't be making eye contact. Not wanting to appear unfriendly to Cowboy's great love, I

217

held out my hand to help her down. Watching her face, I knew she was impressed by the size of Nana Michelle's house, standing proud against the West Texas sky. Heck, even I was impressed at times. With its medical rooms extending out from the south side and its servant quarters in back, my grandparent's place really was expansive . As a kid, I'd sometimes get turned around inside its spacious rooms. I'd have to walk around and around till I found where I wanted to go.

On solid ground, Saint took a few steps forward on the gravel drive. She stared up at the second floor of the house. "Will we be staying here tonight?" I caught a hint of hope in her words. I have to tell you, her voice surprised me, as it was deep and sultry. I had expected her to speak in a girlish tone.

"Yes," I said. "And Johnny, you're welcome to stay too."

Having hopped out on his side, Johnny was already gathering Cowboy and Saint's traveling cases. "Nah," he said. "Going to stop at the lumber supply here in town, then head on home. Still got quite a bit of dust in my house from the storm. Just couldn't keep it out." He fell silent for a moment before adding, "You should've seen Cowboy's father's house. It was practically covered over with dirt."

Cowboy stretched out his limbs and adjusted his rodeo buckle before shaking my hand. "How you doing, Mick?" He didn't wait for an answer. "Johnny was nice enough to take me up to Guymon to check on my dad. That's how we're late."

I knew a few days earlier, another student from Saint's school had given her a ride as far as Johnny Whiskey's place in Dalhart. So I knew Cowboy and Johnny didn't have to go all the way to the middle of Oklahoma to pick her up. I'd wondered what the holdup had been.

Saint spoke, and once again her husky voice surprised me. "It was a good thing we went to check on Mr. Larson. Found him in his barn, covered up to his chest with dirt, with a towel over his face."

Cowboy took the suitcases from Johnny. "He's okay, but he still refuses to move from his farm. Says nowhere else is going to be any better. Thankfully, he's got lots of canned food stored in the cellar."

I thought of the many people who had left their homesteads in search of work. They could be seen everywhere with their few precious belongings piled high on their automobiles or wagons. Going no particular direction in search of work, food, or simply a better situation. It seemed like very few of them were finding what they were searching for. It might be that Mr. Larson was right, but I didn't want to contradict Cowboy.

I turned to Johnny. "Come in and have a bite to eat and a glass of tea, at least."

He hesitated.

"My grandmother's making key lime pie."

He pulled Cowboy's guitar case from behind the pickup's front seat. "That's an offer I can't refuse."

Walking with her head held high, Saint led the way to the front door. Her flowing white dress reached down almost to her ankles. I swear, it appeared as if she were floating instead of walking. My friend Cowboy would have his hands full with this one. My guess was, it would take a lifetime of back-breaking work to give her the lifestyle she wanted. But I wasn't about to tell him my thoughts—some things a person just has to find out for themselves.

Our dogs had run down the gravel drive to greet the guests, and now they stretched under the lone shade tree near the house. Maybe it was the hot weather, or maybe it was Saint's superior attitude, but I noticed they didn't jump up and follow us to the front door. Unusual for these enthusiastic pooches. It was going to be a long car ride to Dallas.

* * *

Enticing smells drifted from the kitchen's screened windows. Nana Michelle held the front door open. "Come in, come in." Her voice sounded vibrant, but physically she appeared pale. However, her cough had eased. It was amazing the recovery she'd made in the short time since the storm.

Inside the kitchen, a big box fan sat near the open windows, blowing toward Josie at the stove. She was working fast, cleaning utensils and pans as she cooked. "I hope you folks like fried chicken because that's what I'm making. That and mashed potatoes, green beans, kernel corn and biscuits."

Nana Michelle's key lime pie sat on the counter. "Mick," she said, "why don't you introduce us to your friends."

"Let's see," I said. "You've already met Cowboy, and this is his girl, Saint. Over here is Johnny Whiskey, the musician that's been helping us find work." I gestured with my hand toward my grandmother. "Everyone, this is my beautiful Nana Michelle and the lovely Josie Polemon, the best cook this side of the Mason-Dixon."

Josie's already flushed face blushed deeper. She brought a heaping platter of fried chicken to the big wooden table. "Y'all, get started before it gets cold."

Cowboy and I dug in immediately, stuffing ourselves as if there were no tomorrow. Johnny ate at a politer pace. And Saint ate tiny mouthfuls she savored ever-so-slowly. Despite her regal appearance, I got the feeling that food may have been hard for her to come by at times. No different from most folks these days.

I watched her trying not to seem like she was looking at Nana Michelle. Nana Michelle, being the ever-polite hostess, tried to make her feel at home. "Saint, what a pretty name. I don't believe I've ever known anyone named that before."

The girl looked surprised at being addressed directly. Cowboy came to her rescue. "Saint is a nickname," he said between mouthfuls of biscuit. "Dove is her given name."

The girl actually looked like a dove, with her soft dark eyes and delicate features. Outside the open window, I heard the moo of a cow. Lucy's bovine head came into view, as she bumped it against the screen.

Josie swatted at the screen with a rolled-up newspaper. "Shoo! Shoo! Lucy, get on out of here!

"Oh, let her be." Nana Michelle said. "Ever since she spent those few days in the washroom during the dust storm, she doesn't want to go back to the barn."

"I don't blame her," Johnny Whiskey said.

"Did those hoof marks come up off the linoleum?" I asked.

"No," Nana Michelle answered. "But it's okay. It gives the house character."

To my surprise, Saint said, "I like you, Nana Michelle."

Even more shocking, she smiled at Grandmother, showing her perfectly aligned white teeth. It was amazing how fast her stiffness had melted away. It was then I realized the girl might've been more scared than haughty. I felt bad for having judged her so fast.

* * *

Next morning, I sauntered into the kitchen where I found Saint standing next to Josie, rolling out biscuits. It was apparent by the amount of work they'd done, they'd been up for hours. The women had their backs to me, so I leaned forward to hear what they were talking about. From their easy laughter, it was evident the two had something in common.

Expertly, Saint used the rolling pin while Josie whipped up some kind of cream cheese.

"The secret is to get the yeast right," Josie said. "It'll make all the difference."

Cowboy entered the kitchen behind me. "What are you two girls making this morning that smells so good?" It was true, the aroma emanating from the oven was heavenly. "You two must have gotten up at the crack of dawn to bake all this."

"I always get up at the crack of dawn." Saint worked as she spoke. "They make us at the boarding school. You should try it sometime —the sunrise is good for the soul."

"Didn't you say they also teach you to sew?" Josie asked. "I just love the Dresden-blue dress you're wearing. You're quite the seamstress; you could make a living with those fine skills."

Nana Michelle came in from the washroom with a fresh set of dish towels. "Good morning, boys!" She slid the towels into a drawer. "Mick, I got the foreman to make sure your grandfather's auto is in good driving condition, all gassed up and ready to go."

Taking the auto made me nervous. I wasn't used to driving nice cars, and this one in particular must have been special to Nana Michelle. PawPa didn't splurge on much for himself, this car being the exception. Even still, I'm pretty sure Uncle Robert gave it to him as a gift. Going over and giving her a little kiss on top of her silver hair, I said, "I'll be sure to get the automobile back to you soon."

"Maybe you can bring that girlfriend of yours for a visit when you bring it back."

I'd never said anything to anyone but Cowboy about being in love with Margaret. "What makes you think I have a girlfriend?"

Grandmother stopped scurrying around and looked at me directly. "You told me."

"No, I didn't."

"Yes, you did. In the song you wrote the other night."

ANTONIA

Sitting among Houston's elite was not my idea of a fun outing.

Everywhere I looked, I saw fabulous hats and pastel fashions, including

the latest hue of taffy pink. Even as the common man struggled to live

another day, our wealthy friends had taken the economic downturn in

stride. To them it meant a few less pairs of shoes, or not buying a fur coat.

Maybe not taking their summer tour in Europe.

Tonight, we were at Lucky's favorite annual charity event, a dinner

to fund the orphanage for another year. He took a special interest in the

orphans, as he was born in an orphanage himself. Soon it would be time

for him to make his grand entrance and give a speech. But first, he

insisted on talking to the children outside—something he did every year.

He enjoyed watching the servants give out all kinds of treats he'd

purchased from bakeries all over the city.

There was no way he was going to miss out on this event, despite

what had happened to Jerome in Dallas. Lucky and the doctor had

discussed the cross-burning for over an hour on a long-distance phone

call. Afterward, he told me he believed it was an isolated incident. But I

remained uneasy.

My husband was a high-profile figure. Some people hated him

simply for the opportunities he'd been given in life. After Mick's

unfortunate front-page photo, I thought we should lay low for a few months—if not years. But Lucky waved my fears away. You're exaggerating the situation, he said. "People know who I am. They won't hold judgment against me."

Glancing around the flower-filled room, I saw people I'd known for years. But I didn't feel like I really knew them. What did they act like when no one was watching? Truly, I felt closer to my cook Juliette than with anyone in this crowd.

Tonight, I'd perceived a slight by two of the women and their husbands as I came through the door with my eldest son André. Their wives angled their shoulders away from us, as if to keep us from coming up to them. André noticed it too, I could tell. He held my arm and steered me toward some of his younger friends. But he didn't linger with them as he usually did. He wanted to be seated at our special table, near the front. The perfect location for people watching.

Everyone looked immaculate, turned out in their finest under the twinkling chandeliers, the last rays of the setting sun casting a golden-pink glow through the huge bank of floor-to-ceiling windows. The white linen table cloths reflected the rose-colored hue. I was grateful André didn't want to talk.

Outside, a chorus of voices shouted Lucky's name in unison, over and over again. My husband was in his element, holding court with the young children and adolescents gathered outside. I heard his familiar voice in response, greeting them. I knew from experience he'd make a short speech outside before coming to the podium inside.

The minutes dragged by as I sipped ice tea and smiled at the few friendly faces in the crowd. André seemed inpatient, drumming his fingers on the table. It made me more nervous, but I didn't have the heart to ask him to stop.

Finally, Lucky entered through the door near the podium, along with Jack Casey and two other tuxedoed men. The crowd inside applauded—though not as loud as the orphans outside had. Clearly, this crowd no longer held any passion for my husband. They were leery of his association with criminals.

The three men beside Lucky held an impromptu meeting just inside the door, their heads bowed in a huddle. Lucky, visibly upset, shook his head. To my surprise, Jack Casey approached the podium and began to speak while Lucky made his way to our table. He sat down between me and our son, giving a tight-lipped smile before adjusting his eye patch. His good eye held a hint of wetness, though no actual tears. Tension radiated from his body. His hand, near mine on the table, trembled. Anger surged in my chest. *How dare they? Didn't they know the thousands, if not millions, Lucky donated to their precious charities?*

Turning to my son, I could see his flashing eyes soften. "Do you want to go?" André whispered.

"No," Lucky said. "I came to this event for the orphans. I intend to stay." I bent down beside my chair to retrieve my purse. No one—especially Lucky and André—suspected what I'd done. The microphone at the podium went dead and Jack Casey's words were silenced.

It would be a good five minutes before the staff realized the cord had been pulled from the outlet near our table. Thankfully, the waiter who made the discovery was a man Lucky had always been kind to when we dined here.

We exchanged a conspiratorial look before he plugged the cord back into the outlet. The microphone crackled back to life. But Jack Casey had lost his train of thought. He looked in my direction before closing down his speech by saying, "Let's eat and have some fun tonight. Thank you for supporting the orphanage. Your patronage is so important to the young men and women just outside this door."

He gave a wave to the crowd as he exited the stage, but his eyes never left mine. I felt certain he picked up the message I was transmitting. *No one hurts a member of my family and gets away with it.*

MICK

We'd not been on the road long when we encountered our first hitchhiker. This wasn't an unusual sight, but Cowboy and I had decided we weren't going to pick anyone up because we had Saint in the car. Besides, our guitars and suitcases took up a lot of room. The plan was to travel all the way to Dallas, switching off drivers as each of us became tired. But this guy was a happy-looking sort and he had a guitar with him. Probably a musician like ourselves, going to his next show. I started to slow, but Cowboy shook his head no. Not enough so Saint could see, but enough that I knew to speed back up and stick with our plan.

In the rearview, Saint seemed absorbed in a daydream. She watched the flat terrain speed by her window. I was glad we had the comfort of an automobile. She wasn't the kind that would make it jumping a boxcar. I smiled as I thought of how Margaret had trouble hopping the boxcars until she finally grasped the concept of grabbing one rail of the outside steel ladder with one hand, and then grabbing hold of the other side of the ladder with her other hand before lifting her feet to climb up and inside. Before she learned this, she'd really struggled. At one point, I practically picked her up and threw her through the opening. No sir, there wasn't anyway that Saint would make it. She wasn't the natural athlete Margaret was.

We'd gone a little way down the road from the point where we'd seen the hitchhiker. For some reason, I couldn't forget how patiently he'd stood by the side of the road, cap pulled low over his eyes, guitar slung over his shoulder, thumb held high. Glancing in the side mirror, I searched for his lone figure on the open landscape behind us. He'd turned from the direction he was hitchhiking and started to walk along the highway's edge, apparently giving up hope of catching a ride.

I wondered how long he'd been on the road. Traffic in this part of the country was scarce. As Cowboy might say, the glamour of hitchhiking drops off pretty fast when you're broke and hungry. And it's downright dangerous if dark catches you without any kind of shelter.

"Should we have picked that boy up back there?" Saint's deep voice disrupted my thoughts. "Look at the storm clouds brewing. He won't have any place to get out of the rain."

I glanced at Cowboy. He glanced back at me.

"His guitar will be ruined." Saint twisted around in the backseat to look at the lonely figuring moving down the ribbon of road behind us.

Cowboy gave a slight nod in my direction, and I slowed to a stop and put the gearshift in reverse.

Navigating backwards, I watched the rearview mirror. The figure jumped for joy, waving his cap high in the air as he ran toward us, and I felt right away we hadn't made a mistake. He was a regular Joe just like us, trying to make his mark. If we all helped each other, maybe just maybe we'd turn this broken world around.

A few feet from him, I moved the gearshift to park. Opening my door, I stuck my head out. "Where you headed?"

"The direction you're going." The stranger said as he came up alongside us. Saint leaned over and opened the door for him to get inside.

"Is there enough room for my guitar?" He looked at the overflowing backseat.

"I think we can manage by sitting it between us," Saint said. I didn't know if she was being kind, or if she was making sure there was a big object between her and the hobo. You never could tell with her. Taking a closer look at the guy, I decided he didn't look like the scary sort. I judged his age to be only a few years older than us—maybe early twenties.

As I started the car and moved the gearshift into drive, I closed my door and we were on our way. "Where you from?" Cowboy asked the stranger.

"Pampa," the guy replied. "Headed out on the road to make money playing."

No one said anything for a few seconds.

Then the hitchhiker continued, "Usually hop trains, but I'm headed to the campgrounds at a lake out this way. It's a little too far from the tracks, so I thought I'd hitchhike. You don't know how happy I am that you all gave me a ride." He stuck his hand up over the seat. "Name's Woody."

Cowboy took the lead. "You can call me Cowboy, everybody else does. And this is my fiancée, Saint. Mick's driving. We're headed to Dallas, supposed to do a show tomorrow night—if we can get there on time. Got delayed by the black blizzard last week."

"Tell me about it," Woody said. "Still shaking sand out of my hair. One of my relatives lost several cows they couldn't get inside in time. Choked to death on the dust."

An awkward moment followed, before Woody changed the subject. His whole demeanor morphed as he told us about the show at the lake he was headed to. Not a regular paying show, like we were talking about. But a show for the migrant workers and homeless people living in one of the shantytown encampments. Woody went onto tell us how important he felt it was to help those less fortunate in any way he could. Said the least he could do was play his songs for them, let them know they're not alone. Make 'em happy for a while.

Saint said that sounded like a real nice thing to do. That she too knew the importance of music when it comes to soothing a soul.

"You guys should come along if you have the time." Woody posed the invitation directly to Saint and Cowboy. I was driving and couldn't turn around, but an occasional glance in the mirror kept me part of the conversation. "It's a big crowd," he continued. "You won't get much money when they take up a collection, but they're a very appreciative bunch."

"When is it?" I asked.

"This evening," he answered.

Looking at me, Cowboy said, "We could probably watch for a little while. Maybe even play if they have a place for us in the schedule."

"If you show up, you get to play." Woody said. "Music is all the happiness some of these folks got right now. They'll stay up all night if someone's on stage."

Up ahead, I could see sheets of rain. As we drew near, a few warm rain drops plopped inside our rolled-down windows, and a couple fell on the dusty windshield. I turned on the wipers and the dust turned to mud for a moment before it was wiped away. Everyone in the car started rolling up their windows, leaving only a small gap at the top for fresh air to enter. It did no good. The windows fogged up as I entered the driving rain.

Slowing to a crawl, we moved along the flat two-lane highway. Far ahead a truck crept along, with furniture piled high on its roof. When the truck turned off on a side road, Woody said, "Follow those people. That's the way to the shantytown."

Almost as fast as the little rainstorm blew up, it passed. We rolled down our windows, pleased to be able to breathe freely once more. "We need more moisture than that," Cowboy said, looking out the window. "But I'm not going to complain. Every drop counts."

* * *

The camp was down by the water's edge in a grove of trees; we would've driven right past if Woody hadn't known how to find it. It certainly wasn't visible from the road. But after we parked our auto in a clearing, we walked down a winding trail that had tents and more autos parked strategically throughout the heavily wooded area. Mirrors, pots and pans, and other necessities needed for cooking or grooming dangled from the tree limbs, giving the woods a magical fairyland feel. As we walked along, we saw small shacks tacked together with wood and metal scraps. I had to admit, these shanties looked sturdier than the ragtag tents some of the tramps were dwelling in.

I tagged behind Woody's solid footsteps. Even though I didn't see anyone, I felt eyes on us as we picked our way down to the water's edge where the concert was being held. I smelled more rain in the air but knew from experience it didn't always come. However, the gusts blowing off the water and the animals rustling in the woods around us told me it might just happen tonight. Hopefully after we played our music.

Woody stopped on the trail. I took a moment to really listen. There's no sound in the world like the hum of the wind blowing through oak trees before a thunderstorm. It was exhilarating. The others around us must have been listening too because there was very little noise except the sounds of Mother Nature.

As we walked along a few people came out to greet Woody. He took the opportunity to introduce us and told them we'd come to play in the show tonight. Some were musicians themselves. They seemed to accept us right away as being part of their tribe, just because we'd arrived with Woody—a man they seemed to have the upmost respect for.

Soon people were spreading blankets over the soft grass and folding out wooden lawn chairs near the water's edge. A few had formal dining room chairs. They'd brought out whatever they had rescued from their homes. I supposed it was better for them to use their good furniture in the woods rather than have the banks take it away with their repossessed houses and farms.

In a beaten down area of the dead grass, a few men were putting up a canvas awning for us to play under. One of them told Woody they were doing it so if the rain started, our instruments would be protected. Woody said it was a good idea. He liked the fact it was not right up on the shore. If lightning struck, it'd probably hit the water.

Someone with an extra blanket asked if we'd like to sit on it. "Oh, it's lovely," I heard Saint say to the woman who'd offered. "Such beautiful stitching." She ran her hand over it. "And quality fabric."

"Thank you," the woman said. "My mother made it for us when we married."

"Surely we shouldn't sit on it," Saint added quickly. "It's practically a work of art."

"I've given up trying to keep nice things nice." The woman laughed. "Look on the back side, it's got a huge stain. Camping is no way to live."

Looking carefully at the woman's face and clothes, I discerned the middle-class gentility she'd left behind. She probably never in her life thought she'd be homeless . . . much less hungry. And honestly, never in my life had I experienced want of any kind. It was shocking to me to see what was happening across the country up close and personal. It had fundamentally changed my perception of how the world worked. I knew my family gave a lot to charity already, but perhaps I could talk them into doing more. Perhaps *I* could do more. For the first time in my life, I realized I'd been leading an entitled existence.

People who weren't experiencing these hard times for themselves rarely had a grasp on how bad the situation had gotten. Take Cowboy, for example. His family had been thriving, growing wheat and corn on their farm. Then the drought happened, and the topsoil eroded and blew away. Suddenly they were dirt poor, scrabbling to get by. Just like this woman and her family, suffering under debts and worries. It was all too much to think about.

I sat down on the woman's oversized quilt and stretched out my legs. Saint and Cowboy were already on their backs, looking up through the tree limbs overhead. I laid back to join them. In the distance, bullfrogs croaked and crickets chirped. From somewhere far off in the distance I heard the mournful sound of a train whistle. Never in my life had I felt so free as I did now, out here on the road. I didn't have words to describe the feeling.

A bushy-tailed squirrel raced along one of the overhead limbs that laced the late afternoon sky. I heard the twang of Woody tuning his guitar and sat up. The gathered crowd already numbered over a hundred, yet they were quiet and respectful, waiting for the show to start. A hushed hum settled over the lakeshore as the people talked to each other in whispers. Someone put a wooden stool under the canvas tent. Oil lamps ringed the makeshift stage.

The sun hung low, making a golden backdrop against the water. Woody began to play. Even the wildlife in the nearby trees seemed to settle down and listen.

When he finished, the people clapped wildly, before settling down to listen again. This time, I watched the crowd instead of Woody. As he worked his magic, their world-weary expressions faded. Excitement lit their eyes as his song transported them to a better place and time. His lyrics gave them hope. Many sang along with every word. Others rocked back and forth, moved by the melody. The love they felt for this musician's message was strong. His very words lifted their soul as he reminded them there was still some hope in this old world.

Caught in his spell, it took me by surprise when he stopped playing and stood up. The crowd called for more, but he put up his hand and told them he had some new talent he wanted them to hear.

He introduced us as Sundown and Cowboy. My heart dropped at the sound of my new name. In a trance, we stood and carried our guitars in the direction of the stage. I felt like I was headed toward one of the biggest musical moments of my life. Little did I know just how right I was.

The crowd parted to let us pass. I heard Saint call out "Good luck!" from behind us. We both turned to look at her, and she blew Cowboy a kiss. I guess we were as ready as we ever were going to be. We'd practiced together on our long train rides and while we entertained our cellmates in the jail.

Cowboy leaned over as we waited for another wooden stool to be brought up. "After we play together, why don't you sing that new song your grandmother was telling me about." I looked at him, surprised. "You know," he continued, "the one you wrote about Margaret."

The sun threw off its last rays, hovering like a fireball over the water. A lake breeze blew over me, ruffling my hair as I tuned my guitar. The water lapped at the shore. I took my place on the stool beside Cowboy.

Looking down, I saw moths being drawn to the oil lamps placed around us.

Cowboy sang first. Then I joined in, just as we'd planned.

Looking up, I felt the love coming toward the stage. The energy of the crowd melded with us, fueling us, electrifying our souls. Many knew the songs we sang, even though they didn't know us. We'd picked popular pieces to win them over. It had been Cowboy's idea, and I must say it was a good one judging by the sea of happy faces.

When we finished, I stepped back and let Cowboy play solo. His fancy fingerwork ignited the passions of those who appreciated superior playing. The crowd whooped as his fingers moved faster and faster until finally the song came to a climactic end.

When he'd finished, he addressed the crowd. "My friend Sundown is going to play a brand new song he wrote about a girl he loves up near Dallas." The crowd hooted. My insides shook. Despite my nerves, I stepped forward with confidence. As I began to play, the words of my song flowed as if sent straight from heaven—exactly in the same way they had the night the melody came to me.

Not too far into my song, a hush fell over the crowd. The sun had slipped behind the water—the moon and the stars had taken its place. I looked out over the crowd to see a few people had lit small fires. The illuminated faces of the young and old, weak and strong, male and female blended together—each thinking of their own special love. That's what motivates every human on the most basic level. Love. The need to give it. The need to receive it.

When I finished, the crowd gave me a standing ovation. Woody and Cowboy stood nearby, clapping wildly.

This is it, I thought. This is what I've lived for all my life.

* * *

The soft cooing of mourning doves woke me. Cowboy and Saint slept soundly on the same quilt we'd sat on at the show. I thought back to the events of last night.

Both of the couple's children had fallen asleep on the quilt next to ours after Cowboy and I finished playing. The music from the next group seemed to soothe them and the woman—whose name I learned was Caroline—covered them with a light blanket and let them stay where they were on the ground. I noticed her husband never quit watching the musicians. He was totally engrossed, and I knew in another life he might have been a musician himself.

The rain we'd been anticipating began, pelting us with big fat drops, and the man stood to wrap up the children and carry them to shelter.

Immediately, we began to wrap up the quilt they'd lent us.

"Let us help you get everything to your place," Saint said to Caroline, who held one of her children bundled in her arms.

The woman nodded. "This way."

We trotted after her and the man, who we now knew as Stephen, to a one-bedroom shack made of wood and tin.

Apparently, Stephen had done some work as a carpenter before the drought. When they'd moved out here to the campground, he found enough good pieces of wood to make a secure shelter. He said he scavenged for days to get the supplies, going through the dump and taking handouts from people in the neighboring town. He'd even managed to get a sizable piece of linoleum to stretch over the wood-slat floor, so the dirt couldn't blow up from underneath.

The shack had one oil lamp on a small table in the middle of the room. A few good dishes and linens lined a homemade shelf on the back wall. I had to admire Stephen's woodworking skills and resourcefulness. While it wasn't much to look at it, this shack was sturdy and dry. A safe haven.

Cowboy took a quick look around before setting off for the auto. "I'll get some of that fried chicken and vegetables your grandmother had Josie pack for us." As I walked him outside, I told him to bring all the food we had for the trip; this family needed it more than we did. Besides, we'd be in Dallas by noon tomorrow. We could find something to eat there.

When he came back and set the big basket of food on the table, Caroline's mouth dropped open. And when we started pulling out everything from mashed potatoes to biscuits and butter, their eldest son roused from his pallet on the floor and looked around. "Am I dreaming," he said, "or is that fried chicken I smell?"

"You're not dreaming." His mother reached for the few dishes she had.

When we were all eating, she tried to mind her manners when everyone else in her family was digging in. Her husband and children gave away just how hungry they were as they shoveled mouthfuls of food down so fast they were hardly chewing it.

Seeing this scenario play out, I decided to eat sparingly, leaving the majority for them. Cowboy and Saint did the same. Now that it was morning, my stomach rumbled something fierce, but I felt good inside.

As I slipped between the burlap curtains serving as a front door, I looked over at the sleeping couple with their two small children on pallets beside them. I hoped we'd brought a little happiness to them with our music and fried chicken.

Out near the water's edge, the sun poked its head up over the horizon, spreading a golden glow tinged with pink over the pristine lake. In the daylight, I could see how far the water levels had fallen. Thank God for last night's downpour. The sound of the rain falling on the tin roof above us had given everyone hope for a brighter tomorrow.

I walked onto a short fishing pier and sat down to meditate on all that was good in the world. It was clear to me a person could endure anything if he had people in his life that he loved. Soon we'd be on our way. I hoped all these people in the Hooverville would find their way back to a decent home and way of life. It seemed like things would have to turn. It couldn't get worse.

When I stood to go, a man approached me at the end of the pier and lit a cigarette. He apparently hadn't been living in one of these jungle camps long, as he was groomed to the nines. He looked more like a Hollywood star than a jungle buzzard in a shantytown camp. His smiling face carried an air of optimism.

"Morning," he said.

"Morning," I shifted my path to go around him.

He touched my arm as I went past. "Say, Sundown, how'd you like to record that song you sang last night?"

His words startled me. He took a draw on his cigarette. "A few buddies and I have a makeshift studio set up at the Vitaphone in Dallas. We're producing new talent." He handed me his business card. I stared at it in disbelief. "Bet you never dreamed a music scout would be sitting in the audience of a shantytown concert."

No, I wouldn't have dreamed that in a lifetime. I realized I'd have never been here either if Woody hadn't taken it upon himself to invite us.

"Thank you, sir!" It was all I could get out.

"You're a good singer. Real good." He turned to leave. "Give the studio a call, and set up a recording session."

He walked back up the trail through the shacks and tents. The birds in the trees lent their voices to this surreal scene. Over his shoulder, the music scout called back. "Bring your friend Cowboy, too. I want to hear everything you two have got."

9 CONFIDENCE & COURAGE

Dallas, Texas

Tuesday Morning

May 22, 1934

MARGARET

Sitting on the bench outside of school before classes started, I took out the letter Jenny Leigh had brought me a few days back. Unfolding the stiff parchment, I turned to the back page and read my favorite part again—the part where Mick said he'd just had a funny thought: *What will we say to our children if they ever ask how we met?*

Indeed, I thought, what would we tell them? Our paths may never have crossed if it hadn't been for my spur-of-the-moment decision to bring Doreen and Bud home. What if I'd stayed late after school that day? Or what if Mick hadn't been bold enough to hop that freight train to follow his dreams? I smiled to myself as I looked up at the bright blue sky, filled with puffy clouds. I prayed a thank you to God for putting us in the same place at the same time on that fateful day. From that moment, my life had never been the same, and I wouldn't have it any other way, in spite of all the heartache.

The handwritten page was starting to show wear. I read the last line. "I look forward to seeing you when I come back to Dallas." His penmanship was perfect, even though he'd probably scribbled it on the train. I'd treasure this note forever. For I was a much better person for just having met him.

MICK

We sat on the roof of one of the downtown brick buildings with the skyline laid out for us in the morning light. "I like Dallas," said Cowboy. "It's a far cry from Guymon, Oklahoma, but I like it. A fella could get used to being surrounded by bars and restaurants. Having store-bought clothes."

It wasn't even eight o'clock, and the day was already warm. Leaning back on one of the wooden chairs the bar owner had put up here, I contemplated the scene below me in the bright daylight. It wasn't so different from downtown Houston, people bustling about as they started the business day. But each city has its own personality, and Dallas was where it was at when it came to music. Unless you were going to go up north to New York or Chicago, or head over to the West Coast, this was the place to be. Soon we'd be going a few streets over to 508 Park Avenue to make our mark on history. We'd driven by it last night just to make certain we wouldn't be late for our recording session.

As I sipped my coffee, Cowboy said, "It sure was nice of the bar owner to let us stay in the upstairs room. Johnny Whiskey hadn't said anything about room and board when he cut the deal for us to play here for a week."

"Probably wanted to get a look at us before he offered the

room." I laughed but feared it might be true. If he'd gauged us to be trouble he might've let us sleep in our car.

We would never have imposed on the doctor and his family for lodging. Deep inside, I knew it would go hard on Dr. Lyles if he was seen around town with me, so I kept my distance. I hadn't even told him I was back yet. I hadn't told Margaret either. I wanted to record our song before I told her about it. There was a superstitious side to me that didn't want to jinx anything by talking about it. Besides it'd be a lot more effective to surprise her with a real recording.

I contemplated just how many nice things people had done for us along the way—things they didn't have to do. I vowed to pay the universe back in some way by doing things for others. Maybe I could do it through my music.

Cowboy woke me from my thoughts.

"Mick," he said. "I need you to know that after this recording session, I'm thinking of trying to get work with the Civilian Conservation Corps."

I didn't know what to say. This is something I didn't see coming.

Cowboy continued, "The government's opening the program to the Midwest states in July. Talked to Stephen about it back at the lake. He told me even though the program was initially for unmarried men like me, they've decided to also recruit veterans like himself. He's thinking about doing it too. Workers get a dollar a day for their wages. That's thirty dollars a month, you can't beat that." His animated face showed me how excited he was about making a stable paycheck. "They send twenty-five back to your family," he said, "and you get to keep five dollars to spend at the camp where you're working."

I twisted around on my chair to look him directly in the eye. "But you don't have a family to support. Why do you want to give up on your dream? Why now, when things are starting to happen for us?"

He bowed his head and took his ever-present matchstick from between his teeth. "I've asked Saint to marry me. Ain't never going to love anyone as much as I do her, and I don't want to lose her. Music isn't stable. I'd be on the road half the time and I wouldn't always know where my next paycheck is coming from. Playing on street corners, juke joints, and country dances ain't no way to take care of a family. And I want a family. A life like my parents had before the drought. A life like Stephen and Caroline have now, even if they do have to live in a shack."

Cowboy was an incredible musician. I couldn't imagine him throwing away his dream. Surely Saint wouldn't let him if she truly loved him. This would work out somehow. No use arguing. Besides, the C.C.C. only let you enroll for work for so long. However, I knew the skills he'd get would probably lead to a full-time job afterward.

It wasn't up to me to tell him what to do with his life. I took a deep breath and rose from my chair. "Let's go cut a record," I said. "Might be the only chance either one of us has to record, so we better make it count."

Cowboy stood and stretched. A yawn escaped and he put a hand over his mouth to cover it. As we went to the fire escape to head back to our room for our instruments, he said, "Last night I couldn't sleep. I was as excited as a little kid about today."

We descended the shaky metal steps. A whistle blew, warning people of a train's approach at the nearby crossroads. The smell of the train's billowing smoke stack took me back to the freedom of being on the open road.

That's where Cowboy and I differed. I yearned to travel and make music almost as much as I cared for Margaret. Somehow, I'd make my two loves coexist.

* * *

We stood outside the big deco building, looking up at the sign. In all caps, the words WARNER BROS. PICTURES • FIRST NATIONAL PICTURES were written in a circle around the word VITAPHONE. It all looked very professional. Very slick. Hoisting our guitars on our shoulders, we headed up to the third floor.

We were ready as we'd ever be. We'd practiced our songs till they were a fundamental part of our beings, including the one we wrote together in the jail at Dalhart. Woody had told us to make sure we came in at three minutes on our songs, so they'd fit a 78-rpm side. It was one of the last things he'd said to us before we parted ways.

Knowing this, I'd asked the owner of the bar to use the sweep second hand on his pocket watch to time us. During the past few afternoons, he'd sat patiently and timed our music again and again, while his waiters and waitresses got the place ready for the evening show in the background. Once again, we practiced until we could get our songs to come in on time.

My stomach tightened as we got closer to the third floor. Cowboy had been playing forever, but I was still pretty new to performing. If Cowboy was worried, he didn't show it. Before we entered the studio, he took the matchstick from his mouth and tossed it in a nearby ashcan. He kind of shook his shoulders and swept back his hair with his hand before opening the door. "You first."

A pretty receptionist greeted us. "You two come to play today?"

Cowboy gave her a winning smile before answering. "Yes, ma'am. I'm Cowboy Larsen and this is Sundown McLaren. We have a ten o'clock appointment to record."

She got up and started walking to the back. "They've been setting up for you."

My palms were sweating as I adjusted the strap on my guitar case.

Please God. Help us pull this off.

* * *

The man overseeing the recording sessions told us to just do our thing as we entered the area to record. "Don't mind all the equipment," he said. "Make yourselves comfortable."

He went on to describe the recording process. He'd need to make two takes of the masters for safety purposes. The masters were made of wax and sometimes one would melt when they sent it up North. I imagined quite a few melted when they sent them through the Texas heat, but I kept my mouth shut.

He asked a few questions about Cowboy's guitar style. I knew there was a guitar solo on the song we'd composed together, and I was glad we'd left it in when we were cutting stuff. It was obvious the record producer wanted to showcase what the talent scout had told him about Cowboy's lightning fingers.

"Are you from Mississippi?" The man said as Cowboy demonstrated a few bars.

"No, sir. Oklahoma."

"Where'd you learn to play like that? You sound like a Delta player."

"I learnt a lot of what I know from my grandfather. He was from New Orleans. Then I picked up some of it here and there from other musicians mostly. That last bit I played, I got from a man named Johnny Whiskey." Cowboy stopped talking for a moment. Then he added, "I can play a wide range of styles including jazz and uptown swing. However, blues is my favorite."

"Then let's play the blues today."

The first recording was our jailhouse composition, "Broken Down Blues." I sang and we both played for the first two verses. Then it was time for Cowboy to show off his fancy playing. He turned to the wall when he played his solo, a technique Johnny Whiskey had called "corner-loading." It did seem to make the sound bigger. Cowboy sure learned a lot from old Whiskey in a short time. As the song ended, I realized I'd been holding my breath. I'm happy to report we didn't embarrass ourselves right out of the shoot.

For the next few hours, we played just about every song we had, doing two takes each time for safety, with only a couple of ten minute breaks.

At one point, the producer came over and said, "Your vocals sound tortured."

I felt a stab of disappointment until he added, "The rawness is powerful . . . those subtle inflections of pitch are going to make you a wealthy man. Keep it up. Let's do one more take."

He waved his hand in the air before heading back to the

recording equipment. "One more," he repeated. "Then move on to the song Mick wrote for the girl—the one our scout heard him sing at the lake."

* * *

In the afternoon, we walked back to the bar. Another group was playing tonight and we could see them setting up. Every muscle in my body hurt as we passed them on our way upstairs. We'd done two takes of eleven songs—everything we'd polished enough to present. Now, we had to wait and see if even one would make it to the radio.

But first, we'd celebrate on the rooftop with Dr Peppers. Then, if we had the energy, we'd probably drag ourselves around the corner to the pharmacy's soda fountain for a burger and fries. And then . . . then I'd call Margaret and tell her I was in town.

Saint was staying with her relatives in Oak Cliff. I offered to drive Cowboy over, but he said not yet. He needed to think over some things first. I decided not to question him further. After all, it wasn't every day a man got a chance of a lifetime.

We'd both done our best with our God-given talents. Now it was just wait-and-see.

DR. JEROME LYLES

I decided to look around the pharmacy while I waited for my prescriptions to be filled. Many of my elderly patients couldn't get to town, so I brought their medications to them on my way home. The pharmacist treated me kindly, but one of the workers in the back stared at me with hostile eyes. Sometimes late at night, I wondered if I should've helped the fugitives. But in the morning's light, I knew I'd done the right thing.

Glancing up at the soda fountain, where they sold burgers, fries, and milkshakes, I was irked by the Whites Only sign near the cash register. Some establishments had integrated after the Great War, but many still hadn't. I closed my eyes and turned my head, vowing not to look at the sign again. There wasn't much I could do about it. Anyway, I had to get the medicines distributed to my patients.

A bell tinkled at the front of the pharmacy, and who should walk in the door but Mick and Cowboy. Last week on a phone call to Nana Michelle, she'd told me they'd gotten work and would be headed back this way soon. She'd told me they probably wouldn't stay at our place so as not to bring more trouble to my reputation. When she said this, I reminded her, it wasn't Mick who'd made me treat the young woman's bullet wound. That decision had been mine and mine alone.

"Hello, Doc!" Mick said as he glanced toward where I was standing at the counter. He immediately headed my way with a big smile on his face. Cowboy followed close behind.

"When did you two get back to Dallas?" I hardly recognized Mick with his slicked back hair and mustache. I certainly hoped no one else did either.

He was jumping at the bit to tell me about his day. I listened as he filled me in on the events surrounding their earlier recording session. The employees at the pharmacy strained their ears to hear too. My spirit overflowed with joy to know good things were coming their way.

Mick asked me about Margaret. Told me he'd wanted to make the recording before he told her about it, as he didn't know if he'd be able to pull it off. That's when I had the bright idea of having him surprise her at the community talent show. She and her sister were scheduled to sing. She'd told Jenny Leigh all about it. I promised to get the details.

Just like that, the worries of my day slipped away and happiness filled my entire being. I had something to look forward to, and it only piqued me a little that the boys went to eat at the soda fountain counter where I could not.

Houston, Texas

Wednesday Morning

May 23, 1934

ANTONIA

We were sleeping late, after staying up all night with Katherine's virus, when Juliette pounded on our bedroom door. I jumped from the bed and ran to see if one of my other children had been hurt. "What is it?" I opened the door to see her standing there with a spatula in her hand.

"Bonnie and Clyde . . . they've been killed. Just this morning, on a back road in Louisiana." Her voice was surprisingly calm.

I felt like falling to the floor. I braced myself against the doorframe. "There wasn't anyone else with them?"

She knew why'd I ask a strange question like that. Anyone else would be puzzled, but not Juliette. Logically, I knew Mick wouldn't be with them, but the whole time he was kidnapped I had feared something like this happening with him and Margaret in the car. I even had a nightmare of such and told Juliette the following morning.

"Come." She held my arm. "The radio reporters are giving details."

Lucky appeared behind me in his robe, pulling his eye patch into place. We descended the stairs to the kitchen.

I could hear the deep voice of a news reporter giving the bare facts as they came into his newsroom. "Seems both Louisiana and Texas law officials set up the ambush, shelling the outlaw's stolen automobile with as many as 130 bullets. After dealing with Barrow for so long, officials did not want to take any chances. In fact, it appeared he was reaching for a weapon even as he was shot." The newsman's speculation made me cringe. My imagination was working overtime.

I looked over at Little Bobby, who was eating oatmeal beside me. He didn't appear to understand what was being said on the radio. I nodded to Lucky to go ahead and turn up the volume so we could hear the reporter more clearly as his voice crackled over the speakers.

"Officers removed a cache of weapons, including automatic rifles, sawed-off semi-automatic shotguns, assorted handguns, and several thousand rounds of ammunition as well as stolen license plates from fifteen states—all discovered inside the notorious duo's stolen automobile as their dead bodies lay nearby." Juliette gasped as she went back to her cooking. Every so often, she glanced over her shoulder at me with a horrified look on her face as more details poured out.

I grabbed my husband's hand. This cache of weapons had probably been in the car with Margaret and Mick. How lucky we were both of them had lived through the ordeal.

My heart pounded in my ears, making me want to drop in a dead faint. Little Bobby sat undisturbed beside me, eating his pancakes. Juliette had put whipped cream and berries on top. He was poking at one of the blueberries with his fork. "Momma," he said. "When's Mick coming home?"

Just then André came around the corner. "Don't you worry about Mick. He'll take care of himself."

"I know," Bobby said with a frown. "But I miss him. He was fun."

Looking at me, André said, "Katherine's fever has broken. She's hungry, can you believe it? I've come to get her some juice and a biscuit."

"I'll take it to her." I needed to make sure she really was better.

"No, Mother, you've been up all night," André said. "Get some rest. I'll stay with her. I've already called in late to the office for both Dad and myself."

In the background, the reporter talked about the multitudes of people showing up to view the bullet-ridden bodies of the dead fugitives. I couldn't listen any longer. I got up and turned the radio off before I left the room. The last words I heard were "G-man's rifle."

MARGARET

The day was stiflingly hot. It was getting on towards four in the afternoon—when Samantha and I were scheduled to sing. I'd thought about backing out this morning when we heard the news about Doreen and Bud—I couldn't bring myself to call them by their real names—but instead I changed the song we were going to sing.

Even though no one else would know, my sister and I would know it was in honor of Doreen—a fine person who'd found herself on the wrong side of the law. To me, Bonnie was a poet, a singer, and a dreamer. And now I would honor her, as I'd promised I would back at the gas station.

When we came out from around the makeshift curtain on the stage, I saw our guitar player sitting off to the side. I'd clued him in earlier we wanted to change our song, and he said he knew the new one. I wasn't surprised because it was an old standard hymn.

Taking our places at the microphone, Samantha reached out and took my hand.

"Hello, everyone. My name is Samantha and this is my sister Margaret. We're going to sing this song today in honor of someone very special to Margaret."

The guitar player started the intro. When it came time to sing, I closed my eyes and let the words come straight from my heart. My voice wavered at first before it caught strong.

There are loved ones in the glory

Whose dear forms you often miss.

When you close your earthly story,

Will you join them in their bliss?

Then my sister sang the chorus with me.

Will the circle be unbroken

By and by, by and by?

Is a better home awaiting

In the sky, in the sky?

I switched to the newer version of the song—the version Doreen and I had sung along with on the car radio as the Carter family performed it live. I heard tell it was the Carter family's daddy that rewrote the lyrics. As I began the verse, I hoped my memory served me right.

I said to that undertaker

Undertaker please drive slow

For this lady you are carrying

Lord, I hate to see her go

Tears choked my singing. Samantha stepped up to sing the chorus by herself.

Will the circle be unbroken

By and by, Lord, by and by

She waved at the crowd. "Join me. You all know the words." Sure enough, the crowd did.

There's a better home-awaatiing

In the sky, Lord, in the sky

I thought of Sister Rosetta telling me I had to show the gift God gave me to the world, 'cause no one was gonna know unless I showed it off. Letting the tears flow down my face, I moved forward to the microphone. As I sang the last verse, everyone in the audience rose and clapped along. Samantha and I sang the chorus as one with the crowd. After all, it wasn't only a song for Bonnie. It was a song for all who'd lost loved ones.

* * *

There were three more acts after us. Samantha and I went out into the audience to watch. Jenny Leigh was sitting with her sister and parents, and she waved us over to their picnic bench. Her mother gave us each a bottle of root beer. I hadn't realized how parched I was until I turned my head back and drained it dry.

The doctor leaned in. "That was beautiful, girls. Margaret, you sing like a nightingale." He had tear-stains on his cheeks. "Only time is going heal all that's happened to us."

Someone tapped me on the shoulder.

It was Mick.

I let out a screech before I realized the other singers on stage might not appreciate the noise. Jumping up, I flew into his arms.

Behind me I heard Samantha say to the Lyles, "I absolutely cannot believe Margaret found a boyfriend before me. And he's a romantic one, at that."

* * *

Later, when we were sitting on the hood of Mick's grandfather's car out in front of my parent's house, I cried real hard as we talked about our time on the road.

"Why'd they have to kill her too?" I sobbed. "I didn't want to go with them when they took us. But I came to understand them, and why they lived like they did in these crazy times. Their frantic search for happiness. Lawd, Mick, I just want to go back and try and change it all."

Hot tears flowed from my eyes in the darkness. My sobs were more like wails, and I was afraid I'd wake my parents. There were no lights on inside, with the exception of one small lamp near the door. Mick wrapped his arms around me and gave me his handkerchief. It was fine linen and had an embroidered "M."

This boy had so much. Why did he care for the likes of me? When I asked him, he said, "You love who you love. And I've loved you ever since I saw you riding like a crazy lady across the Lyles's field." He smiled. "Anytime I'm with you, I feel like all is well. Do you know what I mean?"

I nodded as he dried my tears. He held my face with both hands and kissed me tenderly. I couldn't breathe, partly because he took my breath away and partly because I was still choked up from crying. When he pulled away, it took me a minute to recover. I felt warm and gushy all over, just like I'd read in love stories. I closed my eyes and tried hard to imprint this moment on my memory so I could call it up for the rest of my life.

"Now," Mick said, "let me see that medal they gave you for winning first place." He reached for the ribbon around my neck and inspected it. "Bonnie would've loved that you sang that song for her."

I looked deep into Mick's eyes. "Just think. If I hadn't met her, I'd have never met you."

* * *

When Mick asked me to watch him and Cowboy play at a Saturday night dance, my folks insisted on Samantha going with me. They said they knew how rowdy those dances could get. As we waited by the door for them to come get us, I started having second thoughts. What if we didn't know anyone there? What if no one talked to us? What if we were dressed wrong? I'd never been to a dance. Samantha had once, but it was associated with the school.

Looking out the front window, I saw Mick's auto turn up the drive. Cowboy was sitting in the passenger seat. Between them sat a small slip of a girl. Her dark hair and eyes made a dramatic backdrop for her taffy pink dress. She had a matching bow on top of her head. I'd heard tell you could know if a girl had a boyfriend by where she chose to wear the bow. This girl had it positioned with a hairpin on the right, which meant she was deeply in love. I thought of how Mick had told me Cowboy wanted to get married but his girl wanted him to have stable work first. Maybe tonight would change her mind when she saw how well they played together.

"What are you thinking about?" Samantha asked.

"Nothing."

"Your face is all scrunched up like it does when you're thinking hard."

I tried to relax my face by raising my forehead and bugging my eyes a little.

"Don't do that," she said. "You look weird."

"What do you suggest, Samantha?"

"Stop thinking."

* * *

I shouldn't have worried about knowing people at the dance; the music was so loud it was hard to talk. Samantha, Saint, and I found a small table and chairs up near where the musicians were playing. Everyone else was dancing.

The group on stage had the whole place shaking. Mick and Cowboy were going to have a hard time living up to these players. But I was certain they'd pull it off somehow.

The band left the stage to a standing ovation, and stagehands rushed in and took their instruments, replacing them with two stools they set up in front of two microphones.

Mick and Cowboy stepped onto the wooden platform. The crowd quieted, except for a few scattered catcalls. Without any introduction, Mick began one of the most beautiful songs I've ever heard. Each word rang true, as if he were talking to me. I sat mesmerized.

When he finished Saint leaned over and whispered, "That song is about you."

"How do you know?"

"Andy told me."

"Who's Andy?"

"Cowboy. I call him Andy."

I wasn't used to happiness like this. I held onto it, afraid it might evaporate any second.

A handsome boy came up and asked Samantha to dance. Mick and Cowboy had started a swing number that had everyone up and dancing again. It was at that moment I realized I'd never get to dance as long as Mick was supplying the music. I didn't care. He was more important than dancing.

Saint looked me over carefully, as if deciding if she approved. I tried not to give her cause to dislike me. Her dress was far more fashionable than mine, her features more perfect. Just when I decided she wasn't going to be my friend, she smiled and touched my arm. "Tell me, what do you do about the fans?"

For a moment, I thought she was talking about a couple of big box fans someone had turned on the dancing crowds to cool them down. Several girls were standing in front of them, holding up their hair and letting the air rush over their damp clothes.

Saint gave a little laugh. "Not those fans." She gestured discreetly with her open hand. "*Those* fans."

I hadn't noticed the line of girls to the right of the platform. Some were actually swooning. I'd never seen someone swoon before. Turning back to Saint, I was about to say I didn't like the fans at all, when the song ended and a deep voice boomed. "I know who you are, Mick McLaren. We've been keeping our eye on you. Just because Barrow is dead don't mean you aren't guilty as hell."

The crowd fell silent. Mick didn't say a word.

Some rough looking guys threw stuff at the stage. The fans

screamed and cowered. Cowboy ducked, but Mick sat straight and tall. The crowd laughed when Mick's quick reflexes caught a tomato in mid-air. I thought he'd throw it back, but he didn't He just set it down beside him on the stage.

"Aren't you going to defend yourself?" The bully yelled.

"I've come to play," Mick said. "Not stand trial."

"Don't you think you should be in jail? Or six feet under like your gangster friend?" The bully charged the stage, knocking Mick off his stool. His guitar banged against the wooden planks of the platform as he fell to the ground. It looked like the other man was going to make short work of him. But then, Mick leaped up and knocked him out with a single punch.

He dusted himself off while two stage hands ran forward to drag the unconscious drunk off to the side. Going to the microphone, Mick said, "Does anyone else here want to fight me?"

A few girls giggled. Saint squeezed my hand.

"Good, then let's get back to having fun. Do you want to dance?"

The crowd surged forward. Mick broke into a swing number and Cowboy joined him.

I looked out over the dance floor. Samantha was having the time of her life.

Later, when I asked Mick about it, he just said, "People can believe what they want about me. I know what's true and what's not."

That was what I loved about him. The fact he couldn't care less. I had always cared too much, and it had gotten me nowhere.

* * *

On the drive home, Mick sat in the backseat between me and Samantha while Cowboy drove. Saint sat straight and tall in the front passenger seat.

"Is your guitar okay?" Samantha asked from the other side of Mick.

"Yes." He was silent for a moment. "I have to tell you girls something."

All three of us turned to face him. Saint almost turned her tiny body totally around in the front seat.

"That fight back there was staged."

Samantha gasped. Saint's mouth hung open in surprise.

Mick continued, "We staged it for two reasons. First, to get people talking about us and remembering our names. But there was another reason, a better one. We wanted to see if people were going to hold the gas station robbery against me. The record producer was the one who wanted to gauge people's reaction before he tried to get our songs out on the radio. What with the lawmen ambushing Bonnie and Clyde's car, he didn't know what people would believe about me. And I didn't know what to tell him."

I stared at him.

He continued. "I didn't want y'all to think I was hiding anything from you."

"It was my idea," Cowboy chimed in from the driver's seat. "Saw some guys do it once and it worked out real well for them."

Saint turned in her seat and gave Cowboy a look of utter contempt. Cowboy shot her a smile. "We're in show business, baby!"

Samantha laughed. I couldn't contain myself any longer. Giggles escaped, even though I tried to keep a straight face.

"So the bully, he's not in the hospital?" Samantha said between bouts of laughter.

"Heck no," Cowboy said.

Mick flashed his pirate smile in my direction. "That guy's probably home in bed counting the hours until the bank opens tomorrow morning so he can cash the check I wrote him."

The headlights illuminated the road up ahead. I snuggled closer to Mick's side as I held his hand. I was so relieved no one in the crowd had really turned on him. Still, I had a feeling we were going to have to face questions for the rest of our lives.

"Guess what?" Mick's voice nudged me from my reverie. "We got asked to perform in the Gunter Hotel down in San Antonio next week.

Thought you might like to go with me. On the way back to Dallas, we could make a detour to my parents' house in Houston. I'd like for you to meet them." He turned to Samantha. "Of course, you're invited too. It might make a good summer vacation trip for you two."

In the front seat, I heard Saint say softly to Cowboy, "I thought you were going to give up playing music."

He kept his eyes on the road. "Not just everyone gets invited to the Gunter."

10 DOWN SAN ANTONIO WAY

MICK

The Sunday night air was filled with music from the streets below.

I loved it up here on top of the bar. The owner was kind enough to let us

stay through the weekend because the band that had taken our place at the

end of the week didn't need a place to stay. But tomorrow morning, we

needed to clear out and get on the road to San Antonio.

Cowboy was moody. He'd hardly said a word since we'd dropped

Saint off at the home of her relatives. It had not gotten past me she'd

hardly spoken a word after I announced we'd gotten the gig in San

Antonio. I knew she was mad when we dropped Margaret and Samantha

off at their house. But on the way to her relatives, she didn't yell or

scream. Instead, she put out an icy cold vibe. I knew if Cowboy went to

San Antonio things were going to be over between them.

My friend was stewing over the night's events. Perhaps the two of them could come to some kind of resolution. If not, Cowboy was going to have to make some hard choices. I didn't want to sway him either way.

I peered over the roof's cornice at the street. Down below, a lone saxophonist played on the sidewalk, his velvet-lined case open beside him. In the background, the setting sun shot out rays of gold, blue, and purple, highlighting him from behind. The effect was magnificent, yet haunting.

"Say, that looks like a scene from a movie." Cowboy appeared beside me, pushing his hat back on his head and clamping his ever-present matchstick between his teeth.

The saxophone's wail pulled at my heartstrings, bringing up a deep sadness inside of me. I couldn't verbalize it, but boy I sure could feel it. A young lady came forward and dropped a few coins in the jazzman's case.

A man's voice boomed from behind me. "Who said music is no way to make a living?" I turned to greet the bar owner, an overweight bald man with dark brown eyes that glittered when he spoke. One of his teeth had a gold crown.

"Didn't know you boys were still up here," he said, "it's a perfect spot for people watching, isn't it?"

"Yessir! It sure is." Cowboy turned back into his confident, charming self. No signs of the angst he'd been going through a few moments ago.

The owner walked closer to the brick wall that rimmed the side of the roof. Leaning on it, he looked down for a moment before turning back to us. "Heard you two are headed down to San Antonio. They've got some great places to play, but you need to head back up this way when you're through. I'd be happy to have you play at my place whenever you can."

"Thank you, we'll be sure to take you up on your offer." Cowboy said softly. A far-off sadness filled his eyes, though his tone was upbeat.

The bar owner threw back his head and laughed. "Martin told me you paid him to start a fight at the dance night before last. I may look like a regular businessman in this suit, but I'm a hustler. . . . And I know a hustler when I see one." He pointed at Cowboy. "You, my friend, are a hustler. You and your sidekick are going to go far . . . both got talent and looks. But you, my friend"—he stared directly at Cowboy—"know how to work the system."

His words rang true. What would I do without Cowboy? But I couldn't ask him to stay.

* * *

I'd always hated Monday mornings, but not this one. Cowboy and I were on our way to pick up Margaret and Samantha. They didn't have a phone, but they both assured me they wanted to go to San Antonio. Saint, however, had made it clear she was not going.

As we pulled into the Morningstar's drive, Mollie Belle ran to greet us with a flurry of yelps. Margaret opened the kitchen's screen door and waved to us with a big smile on her face. She held a plate covered in a tea towel. I drove slow over the gravel so as not to hurt the dog, who was near the back wheels.

The screen door opened again and this time Margaret's father walked over to our auto, with Margaret trailing behind him. Samantha waved from the window.

"Mick." Mr. Morningstar came around to the driver's side window I had rolled down. "I like you, son. But I can't let my girls go on such a long road trip, not after what happened here a few months ago. Frankly, her mother is afraid to let her out of her sight. Maybe when Margaret and Samantha are older they can go on trips like this. Do you understand what I'm saying?"

I did. To tell the truth, I had expected it.

He turned to Margaret.

"Tell the fellas goodbye. Then come on back in the house."

Her father walked back up to the house. His work shirt had the sleeves rolled up and I suspected he'd already been up and about doing farm work since before dawn—unlike Cowboy and myself, who'd slept until nine.

Margaret moved close to my open window and pushed the plate she was holding into my waiting hands. "I made cookies for your trip." Her smile was weak and her eyes looked sad. "I'm going to miss you both." Then she looked down at the ground, her hands still on the window frame. "I really wanted to go."

Passing the covered plate over to Cowboy, I put my hand over hers and said I understood.

"That's why I love you," she said. "You always understand." This time her smile was real. She used the back of her free hand to wipe a tear away.

This was the first time Margaret had said she loved me. I opened the car door and got out, pulling her to me. I held her body against mine and kissed her deeply. "I love you so much," I said.

Around my lower leg I felt something swatting at me. Opening my eyes, I discovered Mollie Belle's tail whipping against me as she tried to get in between us.

"I'll see you soon." Margaret pulled away from our embrace. "Or should I say, I'll *hear* you soon when one of your recordings makes it on the radio."

"I told you," I replied. "That's not a done deal."

ANTONIA

The back porch near my garden was my favorite place. I always spent at least a little time out here whenever Katherine and Bobby were preoccupied playing together. Katherine was rallying from the virus. Her color was good, she was eating well, and she wanted to get up and run around. Not too much, I told her. Your fever will return.

In the background, I heard music coming from the open kitchen window. Juliette kept the radio on when she was cooking. I didn't mind, I loved the sound.

"Do you want to have lunch on the patio table?" It was my son André, who was taking the summer off from his college courses. Of course, he still worked several days a week with his father. Today was one of his few days to himself, and I was pleased he wanted to eat with me.

I told him I would love it, smiling to myself as I went back to work on the flowers. I liked having all my family home—well, almost all of it. I closed my eyes and tried to imagine where in the world Mick was on this fine afternoon.

To my surprise, Lucky came outside and joined me near the rose bush I was pruning. It was unlike him to come home from the office for lunch. He didn't say a word as he approached me, just stood and watched me work. A bee buzzed hypnotically nearby. Lucky sighed deeply.

"What's on your mind?" I asked.

He didn't answer. From experience, I knew not to rush him.

Soon enough he said, "Does it bother you we're not members of polite society anymore? I mean, does being slighted at the charity event the other night disturb you?"

Dropping my clippers into a basket on the ground, I turned and put both hands on his arms. "Dear husband, in case you haven't noticed, I was born in Italy. I've always been an outsider here, and I always will be. But I have you, and our family. It's all I need."

"Still," he said. "It hurts to be misunderstood. To lose your reputation."

I carefully considered these words, coming from a former fighter pilot who'd suffered a great deal of physical pain when he was injured in the Great War. It pained me that he had to suffer slander when he'd done so much good in his life.

"God knows your heart," I said. "You do not need to explain yourself to others. Even if you wanted, it would be impossible to go to each person who heard the slander and set them straight."

Holding up the rose he'd plucked, he said, "On a different and better subject, I have good news. Came all the way home from the office to tell you."

I couldn't help but smile as he handed me his rose. "What do you know good?"

"Mick called early this morning. He and Cowboy are playing in San Antonio. They plan to stop in Houston afterwards."

I felt hope swell inside me. "Is he coming back home for good?"

"He's coming for a visit. But that's a start."

André helped Juliette bring the food out to the covered patio. Katherine and Bobby followed. In the background, I heard a familiar voice on the radio—a voice I'd heard singing in the house, in the bath, in the backseat of the car. But now it was singing on the radio in our kitchen.

I looked at Lucky. He looked at me.

"Is that our son singing?" I shouted so loud anyone within a hundred-mile radius could have heard. We grabbed each other's hands and raced back to the house like teenagers in love. That was the thing about our second-born son; you never knew what surprise he was going to bring your way.

Inside, Juliette turned up the volume. Later she would tell me she'd turned up the sound because she really liked the new song. It was only when she saw our beaming faces coming through the French doors that she realized it was Mick.

MICK

"Do you want to drive?" I asked Cowboy after we'd been on the road a few hours.

Never one to turn down an opportunity to get behind the wheel, he said, "Pull over there in the gravel."

I slowed and he opened his door. Immediately, I put on the brakes. "Whoa! Do you think you're riding a boxcar?"

Cowboy shot me a smile and adjusted his big belt buckle before coming around to the driver's side. I got out, and he slid into the seat I'd just vacated.

"Give me a minute." I headed toward a clump of bushes. "I need to answer nature's call."

When I returned two tow-headed boys stood by the driver's side door. Cowboy was giving them the cookies Margaret had made for us. I didn't mind, they looked like they hadn't eaten lately—all skin and bones with too small clothes. "Where'd you two come from?" Cowboy asked. "You live around here?"

"No sir, we're riding the rails with our parents," the younger boy replied. "We got off here to spend the night in a tent by those trees. It's hard for us to sleep on the train."

The older boy spoke up. "Father told us about a man sleeping on top of the boxcar who got pitched plumb off the train when it rounded a curve. So, the family doesn't take chances sleeping inside moving trains anymore. Just on solid ground."

I too had heard stories of people being thrown off trains when the cars maneuvered around a curve. Plus I'd noticed, when I was sitting or standing in a boxcar, the clacking of the wheels made a certain rhythm I liked, but when I was stretched out on my side it was hard to take. I couldn't imagine what it must be like for a little kid.

Cowboy had only given the boys one cookie each, but Margaret had given us two dozen. Reaching into the backseat, I retrieved the rest. "If I give you more cookies will you share with your parents?"

"Yessir!" they chorused. "We'll share with our baby sister, too."

Wrapping the cookies up in a towel, I handed them to the older boy. His face lit up like he'd struck gold. He started to run off, then turned and said in a polite voice that I'm sure his mother had taught him. "You'll never know how much your gift means to us!"

The younger one danced with delight nearby. "Thank you for the cookies," he said. His brother pulled him by the hand back toward the train tracks, where a ragged white tent was pitched under an oak tree not far from the tracks. Inside, I could see a woman sitting on the hard ground holding a baby. She waved in our direction as the boys ran to her.

Going around to the passenger side of the automobile, I slid in and turned down the radio. "Am I glad Nana Michelle let us use grandfather's car. It was rough hoboing on the trains."

Cowboy pulled his hat brim low, shifted into gear, and drove directly into the noonday sun.

He broke the silence. "There was something magical about riding the trains. A certain freedom like I've never experienced before. Now, when I'm near a train and I hear the clack, clack, clack sound, I want to hop on and ride. Not even caring where it takes me. Sure, it was dangerous. Probably too dangerous for those kids and their family to be riding. But to me, it was freedom."

"Tell me about it." I slid on a pair of sunglasses I'd bought at a shop in Dallas. "When I hopped my first freight train out of Houston to come up to Dallas, I'd no idea how it'd change me as a person. For starters, I was so sheltered, I had no idea how many people were riding the rails, scraping to get by. I mean, I knew there were *some* because I saw a movie about it. The film glamorized the hobo life for me. But when I got down near the rail tracks, I was surprised to see more than a handful of people running to get on. I remember, one of them taught me how to hold the handles and swing myself up. Another warned me not to hang my feet over the side when we were sitting with the sliding door open. Said if my feet hit the switch, it'd toss me off into oblivion. Dear Lord, I was so naive it's a wonder I made it to Dallas. Thank goodness I'm a fast learner."

"That you are, my friend." Cowboy turned the volume up on the radio.

Later, as we rolled to a stop sign a four-way crossing, he turned the volume back down. "One thing good that has come out of all these hard times—people coming together to help each other. Just like those hobo kids teaching you the ropes right away. Wanting to make sure you didn't get hurt by some rookie mistake."

"How long can these hard times go on?" I wondered aloud. "Maybe these work relief programs will put more money in people's pockets and pave the way back to a normal way of living. Who'd have thought it would come to this.?" I leaned back against the passenger seat and closed my eyes. "Hard to not feel guilty about all we've got, when so many are suffering."

Cowboy concentrated on the road ahead. "That's the way it is with the world," he said. "At any given time, somebody's on bottom and somebody's on top. All you can do is try to help others when you're on top and hope they'll help you when the situation is reversed." His wisdom always surprised me. He was a regular guy with a lot of common sense, and I was afraid common sense was what I lacked. I also lacked social graces sometimes, and I knew I'd put my foot in my mouth as soon as I asked my next question: "Have you decided whether to quit music for

Saint?"

He didn't answer, just chewed on the end of his matchstick.

"I'm sorry," I said.

"Don't be."

I stopped talking before I got myself in deeper and turned up the radio.

He turned it down once again. "I've been doing this music thing since I turned about twelve years old and am just now starting to see some real income."

Cowboy took the matchstick out from between his teeth and put it in the ashtray. "It hurts me deep that Saint don't trust me enough to let me keep trying."

ANTONIA

My spirits were running about as high as the plane I was riding in. It'd been a long time since Lucky had been spontaneous, though spontaneity was one of the things I loved most about him. It seemed everyday life had beaten it out of him. So when he'd suggested we hop in the company plane and fly to San Antonio to see Lucky perform, I almost came unglued—too much excitement for a mother of four to process! In a short time, we'd arranged for Juliette and Harriet to trade off shifts staying with Katherine and Bobby.

It was a gorgeous day and the hum of the plane's engine reminded me of the day we met all those years ago, when Lucky took me on my first plane ride. On that day, I tried not to talk because I wanted him to concentrate on what he was doing. Today was no different.

"I made reservations at the Gunter Hotel." He turned to me, expecting a response.

I nodded my head. Though I'd never stayed there, I had heard of the hotel by the Riverwalk. It sounded romantic.

"You know that's where Mick and Cowboy are performing?"

I nodded again.

"You can talk, you know."

"I don't want to talk," I shouted over the engine noise. "Just go back to flying." I pointed toward his controls.

We shared a secret smile. He knew I was still afraid of flying. But I'd do it in a heartbeat if it meant I got to see Mick.

MICK

The Gunter Hotel had us set up outside the front door under their covered pavilion, which hopefully meant people coming and going would stop and listen. The bar was also right there, so we had a captive audience. I'd heard tell a lot of scouts watched the acts that played here, and I wanted to impress so we could record more songs.

Cowboy and I had been writing more. In fact, we'd written one together on the way down here. I sure wished I could play as well as him. At least I was born with a good voice. That's the one redeeming thing about me—I could sing well and I've known it since the day I was born. I could tell Cowboy knew he was above par when it came to playing. We made a good team.

Tuning my guitar, I thought of those new electric guitars. They were loud enough you didn't need a piano player to take up the bass line. Speaking of playing a bass line on a guitar, I thought of the *chucka chucka* sound the blues player back on the street corner in Dallas had taught us. It was different from anything I'd ever heard before. And it was something I'd never have learned in a classroom. But I didn't expect my father to understand my line of reasoning.

Across the way was the Majestic Theatre. On the drive down, Cowboy had told me we should keep our eyes open for celebrities staying at the hotel. It was all very glamorous, even if technically we were still playing on a street corner.

Once we were satisfied the microphones were working right. The hotel bartender brought out two barstools for us. Cowboy had to adjust his mic closer to his strings because he was going to be doing a lot more finger picking than me. I kept my mic closer to my face.

It was hot and humid near the river. But the crowds were out in force.

Cowboy decided we should say something about the sailors, as there were so many stationed here. He was always thinking of ways to promote our act, and he had an incredible rapport with audiences. Remarks he made while singing and playing seemed off-the-cuff, when in fact he inserted them every time.

Cowboy was the consummate professional. The years he'd spent playing with other experienced musicians had given him a polished performance I didn't have yet. But I wasn't going to let it get me down. I'd get to where he was in time if I tried hard and paid attention. As my dad used to tell us when we were young, there are some things in life you can only learn by doing. You have to get out there and try. You have to fail before you can succeed.

The first song we played was the one we wrote in the jailhouse out in West Texas. It had a fast rhythm and an instrumental, where our guitars answered each other. Outside of the song I'd written about Margaret, it was one of our best.

People responded immediately to the music, coming forward to watch the show. Before long we had a small crowd. Up front stood a group of real pretty girls. One of them had eyes dark as coal, and they flashed not unlike Saint's. I wondered if Cowboy had noticed her adjusting the colorful flower over her ear or tossing her luxurious black hair. To turn a phrase, she stood out in a crowd.

The crowd grew larger. She and her friends moved closer to us. When I took the stage solo to play the song about Margaret, she motioned with her finger for Cowboy to come over to her. I couldn't hear what she said but it still made him smile. She placed a little kiss on the side of his face and left a red lipstick mark. Maybe it wasn't going to be as hard to get him to stay on the road as I thought it might be.

Out of the corner of my eye, I saw the bartender step outside. He was nodding to the music. I took this to mean the management was happy with our playing. Almost as soon as he came out, he went back inside. The bar was overflowing.

The lights from the surrounding stores and restaurants gave everything a festive look. I loved the tropical feel of this part of the country, especially when the sun went down.

All too soon, it was time to wrap things up. Between us, we'd played just about every song we knew—some we'd written, and some popular ones we knew the crowd would recognize. When I was on stage, I felt electrified. I was sad to see the fun end.

As we finished, Cowboy stepped to the microphone and reminded people of our names. The last thing he said was, "We've recorded some songs, so listen for us on the radio."

My first thought was he shouldn't be telling them that until it was a reality. My superstitious self didn't want to jinx it.

He continued, "This young lady over here told me she heard our jailhouse song 'Broken Down Blues' just this morning. Now, I don't know if that's true or not, but she has no reason to lie." He smiled at the girl, and she gave him a sashay and a flip of her hair.

Another woman moved forward through the crowd, shouting in an Italian accent. "It's true! We heard the song, too!" She pulled a man by the hand along behind her. My brain couldn't process the improbability of it all. First that our song had actually been played on the radio, and second that my mom and dad were standing before me beaming with pride.

The crowd surged around us. I caught Cowboy's attention. "Hey, that's my mother."

"You mean the real pretty lady that spoke up last?"

"Yes."

"Man, I felt sure she was one of them celebrities I've heard stay here."

I elbowed him to quit talking. My parents were pushing their way toward us. As I greeted them, they told us how they'd decided to come on the spur of the moment to see me play. In all my life, I'd never seen them so carefree, or at least not since before they began Katherine's polio treatments. It made me feel good to know I'd brought some happiness their way. I noticed my mother had also bought a colorful flower to put in her hair.

"Please come up and see the incredible view from our suite," she said. The bartender came out with some sandwiches and ice-cold sodas. He said we earned it for the way we played tonight.

I was flying high on adrenaline and having more than a little trouble coming down. Judging by the stupid grin on his face, Cowboy was too. "Let's take this food up to your room," I said. "Our room's the size of a broom closet."

"But we get to stay for free!" Cowboy added. "So, we're not complaining."

* * *

The windows of my parents' suite were open and I could hear the street noises below. In the attached sitting room, Cowboy and I were sitting at a table with my father while my mother snoozed in the other room. He'd brought out a bottle of whiskey and poured a few glasses for a toast.

"Wait," I said. "You have to use grandfather's favorite toast."

"I almost forgot." Dad cleared his throat. "To Cowboy and Sundown's success." Glasses clinked. "'Tis good," he said.

"'Tis good," I chimed back.

Cowboy used his best Southern accent. "'Tis good we didn't embarrass ourselves tonight."

I began to harass Cowboy about the pretty girl he'd been talking to during the show. Slowly but surely Cowboy started to talk about Saint and how she didn't want him on the road, how she wanted him to take a stable job and settle down. I could hear the pain in his voice as he said he was on the fence about what to do.

I slurred a little from the liquor when I blurted that Cowboy should forget about Saint if she didn't support his dream.

Then my father spoke. "Let me tell you two something," he said. "My birth mother was January Buchanan."

Cowboy choked on his whiskey and turned to me. "How come you never told me this before, partner?"

"I didn't know myself." I was shocked. My brain couldn't process this new fact of my heritage. "Dad"—I had to restrain myself to keep from shouting—"why haven't you ever mentioned this before?" I was absolutely dumbfounded that I was related to the renowned singer. She was a legend.

Lucky didn't answer right away. When he did speak, his words were slurred, too. "She left me in an orphanage so she could pursue her career, instead of starting a family with her one true love—my biological father."

Suddenly it was very clear to me why my dad didn't want me following the same path as his mother. Why he'd fought so hard against my dream had never made sense to me before tonight.

My father continued: "Cowboy, you shouldn't let blind ambition keep you from the things that matter in life. People matter. Not wealth, not fame. My birth mother, January Buchanan, died alone in a hotel in Europe. I hardly felt a thing when her manager notified me of her passing. In truth, I'd never known her. She was as much an enigma to me as to the rest of the world."

My mother appeared at the bedroom door. In the low light, she watched the three of us.

"I have a thought." Lucky held up his whiskey glass. "Cowboy, I could get you on with our oil company division in Dallas. I know our regional office is doing a little better than others. I'm sure I could find something for you. It would be a good fallback if your singing doesn't work out."

I moved forward in my chair. "But Dad, he needs to put one

hundred percent of his energy into making the music career work." My words surprised me. Clearly I was as driven as my grandmother January.

"No, Mick," Dad said with a hint of anger in his voice. "Cowboy can do both." He let his point sink in. Then, using my own words against me, he said, "You need to let him make his own decisions."

He turned to Cowboy. "I can set up an interview for you with the foreman next week. You'll have to start at the bottom. I won't lie to you, it's hard work. But you can move up fast if you're good. Lots of men are vying for a job like this, so don't turn it down too fast."

I got up and went to look out the window. Instead of starting an all-out-yelling-match with my father like I usually did, this time I simply changed the subject. "I heard tell, some businessmen are going to put shops and restaurants on the Riverwalk. Going to make it a big attraction for locals and tourists." I took a sip of whiskey before continuing. "If they can pull it off during these tough economic times, I think it's a great idea."

My dad's defensive pose melted away. His shoulders relaxed and the anger left his voice. Taking his cue from me, he let his anger go and didn't pick it up again. "I think those businessmen have a great idea too. Maybe we should look into investing."

It was at that moment I realized my father and I were more alike than I'd realized. We were both fighting to show our worth to the world.

To leave our mark.

* * *

The drive home was uneventful compared to the two days we'd spent in San Antonio. I loved the music, the atmosphere. We even got to see the Alamo. Can you imagine that? The Alamo was just down the street and around the corner from our hotel.

Without a doubt, I liked traveling and encountering places and people I'd never seen before. Perhaps, like my biological grandmother, this need for adventure was in my blood. Maybe it was in my dad's blood too. After all, he'd signed up to be a fighter pilot in the Great War at the age of seventeen, in spite of his own father's protests. Whatever the case, I knew one thing for certain—I liked to roam free. As Cowboy said, there's nothing like the freedom of being on the open road. Nothing else compares.

Cowboy hadn't said another word about it, but I knew my father's job offer was weighing on him. He probably didn't want to let me down.

"Maybe you should interview for the job," I said.

He adjusted the matchstick between his teeth. "I was thinking I might. I don't mean this to be disrespectful, but you've got to remember I don't have a wealthy family to fall back on as a safety net. In my family, I am the safety net."

I didn't answer. I'd never known how it felt to live on the edge like he'd been doing for the last few years. That wasn't my lot in life. Our family had a whole different set of problems, like Katherine's polio and the ups and downs of our oil business.

We drove in silence until a mirage appeared on the road ahead of us. "That's always a strange sight to see," Cowboy said. We knew it wasn't really water on the road. Looking out the car window, I saw the landscape had become much less tropical than it was near the coast. Cedars and oaks dotted the fields along the road.

"Should we stop in Austin for lunch?" I said.

"Austin sounds good." Cowboy said, taking the matchstick out of his mouth. "There's a barbecue place I know—"

He stopped short and turned the volume on the radio way up high. It took me a split second to understand what was happening.

I have to tell you, there's nothing in the world quite like rolling down the highway and hearing a song you wrote playing on the radio.

I couldn't wait to tell Margaret.

MORE BOOKS BY GINA HOOTEN POPP

The Storm After (Winds of Change Series – Book 1)

Lucky's Way (Winds of Change Series – Book 2)

The Emigrant's Song (Winds of Change Series – Novella)

Chico Boy: A Novel